# Synthetic Sanity

Caroline C. Cole

**This book contains occasional profanity, subtle drug use, sexual content, and brief depictions of both gore and death.**

This is a work of fiction. While some places, characters, and history may be real, this is a fictional book and resemblances are coincidental. Opinions are that of the character not the author.

New Young Adult Fiction

You can learn more about the author and her books at the following websites:

carolineccole.com

www.facebook.com/carolineccole

instagram.com/caroline_carter3

Cover photo by Mattie Cagle All rights reserved.

## ACKNOWLEDGEMENTS:

Thank you to my insanely talented cover artist, Mattie Cagle. I am so grateful for you and all of your hard work! Who knew taking ugly selfies in Freshman year gym class would lead to a lifelong friendship. I love you, and I am so glad we are better at making decisions now.

Check out more of her artwork on Instagram:

@mattiecagle.wha

## DEDICATION:

To my brothers for being my best friends. To my friend William for being nice to me on my first day at a new school. To Rupert Grint for playing Ron Weasley, and more than anything, to my momma for never letting me feel crazy.

No matter how much I write, I will never have the adequate words to describe my love for you all.

# CHAPTER ONE: INSANE

Raise hell, eat cornbread. This redneck has a tattoo that reads "Raise Hell, Eat Cornbread" sloppily placed and glittering with beaded sweat on his pointy collar bone. I wonder if I am beginning to hallucinate from the hot sun beating down on me. Surely this level of inhuman ignorance is impossible, right? I start to fiddle with my honors medal, nervously, as I try to comprehend what would compel someone to go through physical agony so that they can have a damned place paired with a popular side dish engraved on their body for all eternity. "June Wilson" my mind is swiftly yanked back to reality as I realize it is time for me to stumble across the stage. My stomach churns at the thought of engaging in a sweaty handshake with my obese principal, but I swallow back the bile and do what is necessary in order to be handed my little mock diploma. As I flash a pained smile for the eager photographer, I realize no one is cheering for me. Deep down I know my family is perched on those bleachers weeping for somebody else. Someone who is able to steal my spotlight despite being six feet underground.

Ages later, the final person's name is called. Eufaula High School's class of 2005 is released like guard hounds. Our mission being: locate our family while consistently making shallow small talk with the people we have tolerated for the past four years. I am thrown into what seems like a thousand pictures with my peers, some of whom have barely uttered two words to me in the past. Through the haze of jittery classmates and their adoring parents, my eyes somehow manage to land on my brother Jamie's outline. I attempt to uncoil this random jock's arm from around my neck, accidentally knocking down the girl on the other side of him in the process. Annoyed, she shoots a crude comment in my direction. I almost feel an unsettling mixture of guilt and embarrassment before remembering this is the last time I will see the troll.

I run to my brother and he bear hugs me as if he has not seen me in eight months, oh wait, he has not. My brother enrolled in the military two years ago, right after my sister, Elizabeth, was killed. When I really miss him, it is hard to remember the point to his lifestyle. Jamie's not extremely patriotic nor does he have an overwhelming desire to help others. Every time I ask him why he joined, he simply shrugs indifferently. He just wanted out. I cannot blame him. *Who could?* You do what you have to do to keep from rotting in self-pity.

I feel my heart plummet as I reel back from his embrace and realize my mom is not amongst my other family members. My oldest sister, Addison, sees my eyes swimming in hurt. She immediately begins combing her fingers through my hair and pleading with me not to be upset with my mother.

"It was just too much for her, sweetie. It was pretty surreal for us all. She just needed a minute to herself," she offers as an excuse. I take a deep inhale and slowly nod my head. I swallow back the incoming tears hard as it sinks into me that this is something I will never forgive her for.

Later that night at dinner, I begin shaking. I cannot suppress my anxious excitement a moment longer. All six of my immediate family members are finally present, our clan chewing stale bread in what has to be Alabama's most crowded steakhouse. This will make it near impossible for the rowdy bunch to cause a scene. I relish in that smugness for a moment before calling attention to myself with a crisp throat clear. As their interested eyes gaze at me, I feel butterflies awaken in my nervous stomach.

I need to tell them about my summer plans in a precise and well-thought-out manner. I am going to explain to them how taking an internship at Maze Estates, a respected hospital for the mentally insane over in Tuscaloosa, will be beneficial to my future career as a clinical psychologist. I have to emphasize that the ancient, maroon-toned brick building only looks dilapidated from the outside. That the environment within is clean and sterile. I will make sure to explain that Maze's strict rules and regulations ensure safety for all of its employees, whether they room there or not. That part is especially important because I will be living within the actual institution for two months.

Unfortunately, all of this projects out as jumbled word vomit. I feel so much pressure to explain everything perfectly, that I somehow make the internship sound partially like a child's nightmare and partially like a twisted joke that only I find funny. At one point, I even reference zombies because the patients are not fully aware of what is going on. I manage to make my summer plans sound like a voluntary apocalypse. *Sometimes I question my own sanity.*

My family immediately erupts with protests. I sit there and tolerate their complaints for a solid ten minutes. They are making sense, and I resent that. Soon I find myself perched on a toilet seat in the restaurant's bathroom. As I sob into a wad of generic tissue, I cannot help but double guess my own upcoming plans. Perhaps, my family is right; maybe this is unsafe. Perhaps, it is selfish of me to abruptly leave my mother and younger sister, Delilah. My mom does deserve time with what is left of her children. Then again, I deserve time away from my utterly unstable family.

My presence would be more of a figurehead. It is not as if my mother would actually spend time with me, she never does anymore. Delilah threw herself into religious practices after Elizabeth died, and she will be too involved with her church's vacation bible school this summer to notice my absence.

I wipe the last of the mascara residue from my face and walk back to my family's table. To my surprise, only Jamie remains. My brother informs me that he asked everyone else to leave and had assured them we would be home soon. I am caught off guard when, on the drive back, his silver economy car pulls into an empty hardware store parking lot, and he reaches across me to the glove compartment. He yanks out a small bag of weed along with a keychain pipe.

Jamie claims he bought it before his last leave. The guy who sold it to him advertised it as the "best shit he'd ever tried." We look at each other and start to giggle, knowing it will only be high-mids at best. As he takes the first hit, I cannot help but continue laughing as I imagine how in the world he is going to pass his next drug test.

A slew of coughs and a couple of hours later, we pull into the driveway of my mother's plain, two-story house. Jamie shifts his gaze over to me, a solemn tone in his scarlet-red eyes. I feel all the moisture leave my mouth. "Do you ever not miss her, June?"

"Yes, all the time." I quickly reply.

"No, I said not." I refrain from making eye contact with him. The car door slams behind me as I stalk into the house, up the stairs, and into my bedroom. I had heard him crystal clear.

# CHAPTER TWO: CUCKOO

A week breezes by, and I am more than ready to get going, well, almost ready. Okay, it is the night before my departure and I have not packed so much as a sock. I run worried fingers through my frizzy, copper-toned hair as I whiz around my room throwing articles of clothing into my bags as if I am at a superstore on Black Friday.

"Just get lots of clean underwear, and you'll be okay." I murmur to myself as I try to keep my panic levels in check. At around 3 AM, I call it quits. I secure the last zipper on my oversized suitcase and try to enjoy my last time sleeping in a queen-sized bed for the summer.

My alarm goes off early the following morning, blaring a remarkably obnoxious ringtone. *You know that sound that makes you want to murder your neighbor in cold blood?* The realization that I have thirty minutes to get ready rushes to my head. I have no choice but to execute my routine in stellar time. Seriously, I could have placed in the procrastination Olympics. Just bronze though as I would be too lazy to walk up another two steps for gold.

The sprint to my little red sedan, bags in tow, is intercepted by a greeting from a strange man sitting at the kitchen table. He is studying his cellular with intensity as he shovels off-brand marshmallow cereal into his mustache-framed mouth. Okay, he is not a complete unknown. I have met him, and then seen him again from time to time as he was picking up my mother for dates. I am on the verge of positive that his name is Christopher. I vaguely remember that he is a contractor taking a "breather" from his career.

Regardless, why is this supposed Christopher, comfortably eating in my home? More importantly, how did he get that particular cereal into this household? I find cat food infused with freeze-dried hunks of sugar revolting. I resent Christopher for making me nauseated on such an important day. I simply give the intruder a head nod before yelling for my mom.

She bursts through the door and to my dismay, immediately skips to Christopher and places the sloppiest of kisses on his stubbly cheek. My entire mind and body seize into a subtle but fully felt cringe. She then deems it appropriate to acknowledge me. I interrupt her before she can speak, reminding her I really have to get going.

This brings forth the tears. I expected she would engage in the whole charade, so I am not the least bit phased. I reassure her of my safety and how the internship is crucial to my future. My mom replies to this by softly saying, "I know. I just love you."

Though simple, her statement sets off a sensation in my body that causes me to feel as if luke-warm bath water is spreading through my veins. I guess you can also describe this as that "touchy, fuzzy feeling". Emotions are hilariously bipolar. I can be narcissistic all day, every day, and something will happen or be said that just makes me feel bigger than myself. I push resentment aside and lean in to hug my mother tightly.

I reel back from her just as Delilah sulks into the kitchen. She gives me a speech, the kind that has obviously been pre-planned, and probably rehearsed in front of a stuffed animal audience. I half-listen to her, mostly because she is horribly boring, but partly because I am jittery and really, really ready to get the hell out of my house.

Eventually, I interrupt her rambling. "Yep, that all sounds great Lila. I'll be sure to convert some heathens. On the other hand, I suggest you try to sin a little while I'm gone. Loosen up, let some actual personality surface."

I respond to her ensuing, blazing glare with a light-hearted wink and a peck on her chubby cheek. I give my mother one last squeeze and throw a 'you're unimportant in this scenario' glance at Christopher. Then I grab my keys off the granite countertop and power walk to my car.

As I back out of the driveway and onto my road, a garbage pop song featuring a nasally female voice booms through my speakers. I swiftly seek through stations until the melody of a catchy 50's tune fills the enclosed air. A song that new-age artists cover and make listeners think is original material. This happens to many great tracks from decades past. I prefer to listen to older music because the lyrics have actual value. The thought behind them is inspiring, at least the writers were attempting to make a point. You could say I am an old soul in that sense. I would not pin me as that into music though. I have always preferred to watch TV. They say seeing is believing, so I guess I can buy people's bullshit a little more when I see it rather than hear it.

Tuscaloosa is only about three hours away from my hometown, however, it seems substantially farther as I drive along the flat, winding roads. With every ghost town I pass, the knowledge that Alabama may in-fact be Hell on earth sinks further and further into my mind. It's just so undeniably depressing. I do enjoy driving though. I cannot distract myself with mind-numbing television or internet. Driving forces me to actually develop thoughts.

On the way there, I am unable to refrain from pondering over how leaving my family for almost the entire summer before I actually depart for college, and then transition into an independent adult, will affect our already strained relationship. My senior year was the last time I would be living in my hometown with the people I have known since birth. This phase has come to an indefinite close. The average graduate prolongs by staying at home for at least the remainder of the summer, but not I. I am pursuing the grand escape.

For a brief, fleeting moment, I actually think this decision may result in regret. I almost giggle when I recall that I have not even been living with my real family. They no longer do, and never will embody the dynamic I grew up knowing.

In fact, this pitiful attempt is far from our original stance. I was raised within what society deems as an above average-sized family. This made for a refreshingly, open environment. I could always persuade one, or more, of my siblings to play with me. There were enough of us to form teams, which made games a lot easier. We had enough personality traits to balance one another out and make sure nobody felt overlooked. As most large families, we did everything on a grand scale; holidays, meals and feuds. My family could get loud and intense, but we had so much fun.

If my parents did not take care of something for me, my siblings would. Overall, we were strong. When I was ten, circumstances began to change. My family began its decline until reaching its heartbreaking demise. Apparently, our group had surpassed its expiration date.

Sure, lots of people get divorced. Heck, half of marriages end in divorce. That's not the biggest altercation for my family. I did not then, and still do not, care that much about my parents' decision. In my opinion, indefinite separation is not a taboo. Everyone deserves to find their happiness at some point or another. The real problem is getting married prematurely or under false pretenses. The only factor that should compel a person into marriage is experienced love. That sounds horribly cheesy but bear with me.

An unplanned pregnancy, a money issue, or lust should not rush you into exchanging vows. If people paced themselves, and only turned developed relationships, that have withstood a substantial amount of time, into marriages then maybe we could cut down on divorce rates. It is not that people do not value the sanctity of marriage anymore. The issue is that past generations did not value it enough to build a lasting foundation before making such a commitment, thus fabricating a corrupt social standard bound to failure.

Again, my parent's divorce did not phase me too much, but it was the marker of the start of my family's deterioration. A divorce does mess with everything, and there was a brief time where all my siblings' opinions varied. Resentment was the primary feeling towards our parents. Soon, my family fabricated a new normal. At that point, all of my siblings and I stayed in the house we had all grown up in with my mother. My dad was the only member to move out. We were never incredibly close, really, he is a distant man who keeps all his children at arm's length. His absence was not all that noticeable.

The following year, Addison went off to some community college near Gulf Shores. Now her departure, that created a rise. She had often split the role of mother with my mom, so her leaving made the other four of us feel lost. We matured as a coping mechanism. If my siblings and I wanted to continue our usual routines, we would have to gain some independence because Addison was not home to baby us. We dealt with this new way of life for about three years before Jamie too abandoned me, Elizabeth, and Delilah.

He did not leave for the military right away. Oh, on the contrary, he made the substantial mistake of accepting a low-income job and moving into a moldy apartment, it literally reeked of decay and mildew, with his high school sweetheart. This baffled me because he was my most valued ally. We bonded together in most family disputes and had each other's backs the majority of the time. I was disappointed in his choices, to say the least. Addison's absence made the house lack warmth, and Jamie's made the house lack security. Two things present in most well-balanced homes.

The big doozie that blew our family to smithereens was, of course, the death of our beloved cat, Chobani. I have no clue if we will ever recover from such tragedy. Shit, did I say cat? I always do that. My bad, I meant sister. *Alright, alright sorry.* I have some serious issues, including comedic suppression.

Chobani's not real; I would never even name a cat after yogurt. I just feel like going straight for Elizabeth is a touch too heavy. My inappropriateness aside, Elizabeth's death was what definitely annihilated our family dynamic. She stole the fun. Elizabeth was always the energetic, lively one. I would often catch her twirling down the hallway or singing off-key in the kitchen. At times, I found her behavior obnoxious, but after she was gone, I realized what an uplifting role she had played in my life.

My once vibrant home is now some type of pathetic, empty shrine. It took so long for me to be able to walk into any room in the house without being flooded by heart-wrenching memories. Sometimes, I really wish the damn building had just been sold or, better yet, torched. My mom thought it would be too painful for me and Delilah to lose yet another stability in our lives like our home. In her mind, Elizabeth was on the brink of moving out anyway. Her not living with us is not a substantial result of her death. For me, trying to remind myself that she would have been away at college is a moot point.

It is not her absence in the house that is so damn hurtful. It is the memories lurking in every crevice that result in a suffocating body and aching mind. My father moved to a new house Elizabeth had never entered for this very reason, and he had not even been living in our childhood home. I try not to judge my mother's way of grieving, but I cannot wait to sleep in a room, in a bed, that my sister has never been in.

A few wrong turns later, *haha get it because I am in inbred nation*, I finally arrive at my much-anticipated destination. *Oh. My. God.* I rack my brain for the reason I wanted to go to Maze. It is an asylum. Like truly, an asylum, with mentally disease-ridden patients. You imagine it, but no you cannot comprehend what Maze is like in reality. I know I could not until I drove up and saw them. I begin hyperventilating as I realize the glare from the sun on my car is creating a shimmer, and they are probably attracted to shiny things. I'm kidding….

Sort of.

The patients are collectively walking around the lawn, sporting vacant expressions. The moment my vehicle deviates from the main road and rolls across the worn gravel, they all turn to look in a single fluid motion. Every. One. Of. Them. *I am living in a horror movie.* No, seriously, I am not being a drama queen. My lip is quivering, and my hand is shaking in fearful discomfort.

All I can figure to do is muster a nervous laugh and wave at the hungry looking patients like I am Miss America. This sounds ridiculous, but I am panicking. *What the hell am I supposed to do?*

I pull into the virtually empty lot behind the building and trundle over the rock fragments to a bouncy stop. Only about twenty cars are parked in the enormous space. I should have anticipated this. It is not like the patients can drive. Still, it is eerie. I feel as if a cold vapor is consuming my chest as I realize I am completely alone. I will walk into the institution and be surrounded by unfamiliar faces. Many of which will be undoubtedly unfriendly.

After the smallest of panic attacks, I switch off my engine and crack open my door. Gathering all of my luggage, along with my purse and cellular, in my two feeble arms is quite the struggle. After I finally seem to wedge everything into a reasonable position, I slowly trek around to the front of the building.

The only thing that remains in the yard is the weeping willow that rests on the far right, its delicate branches swaying slightly in the breeze. Playtime has come to an end. All the patients have been herded indoors. Maybe the employees did this for my sake. If so, I am beyond grateful.

I hobble up the entrance's creaky steps. The big, cherry-wood door swings open just as I am confusedly attempting to figure out how to buzz myself in. A short, sturdy woman surfaces. She appears to be middle-aged, 47 is my guess. She has a faded auburn mane and tired eyes accented by crow's feet. She looks past me, focusing on my heavy luggage, while an aggravated smirk plays across her face. With a sigh, she says in an abrasive tone, "oh God, above. There's another intern."

My teeth immediately pierce my tongue to keep me from spitting back, "No shit, you orangutan." Instead, I offer a pleasant, yet businesslike, grin and let out a chipper, "yes ma'am" as a proper, little southern girl should.

The burly creature grunts an invitation to come in before introducing herself as Miranda Robinson. I follow her into the open foyer. I zone Miranda out for a moment as I absorb my surroundings.

My reflection glittering off the sparkly white floors I am standing upon catches my eye. The distinct sound of typing drifts to my ears, the cluster of offices to my right being the source. Opposing these cubicles is a monstrous curved staircase that leads to a slender catwalk. The catwalk is met at either end with hallways. Hiding behind these insanely enormous stairs is a sunroom. In it are three granite colored sofas angled at a conservative-sized television. A smudge-covered glass coffee table separates the entertainment from the seating. In all honesty, the place resembles a nursing home void of sharp edges.

My attention is awoken by the sound of a crisp snap.

"Helloooooo?" Miranda asks. I persist in continuing to scan the premises for one more moment before giving in and locking eyes with her. I am curious, issue me. Once I mutter a "sorry," she resumes her spill. Which takes a more serious turn than anticipated.

"Okay, honey, so I'll be blunt. This place can be scary, and it can certainly get a little wild. If you manage to hold onto your sanity throughout the summer, you will have succeeded. You are cute. The guys will look at you. They will make some comments, especially considering your chest size on that little frame. Ignore it. If they touch you, report it. You and the other two interns are staying on the third floor, so you won't be neighbors with the patients or anything like that.

"Some of the patients and their guardians have already consented to let the interns sit in on their sessions with Dr. Mosh and Dr. Brooks. Some want to meet y'all first. Of course, you're going to need to sign the forms and all that nonsense. These offices to your right are where you can take care of it all. We eat three times a day in the cafeteria, which is an add-on to this floor. It's down the hall to your left, make a sharp right when the hall ends, and you're there. But of course, Lacey, who you are shadowing, will show you. If you need other things, like snacks, soap, tampons, we have a small store behind the cafeteria. If you need something more substantial there is a Wal-Mart about 15 minutes west.

"Like I said, Lacey will be your supervisor. She is our newest nurse. She will be by to grab you once she's done with midday rounds. Lacey is super sweet, but beware, she can be a little ditzy. Well, you are young. I'm sure you can be, too. I think I have covered all the basics. If you have further questions, save them for Miss Lacey. You can head over to the first office on the right and check yourself in… Oh and enjoy your stay here at Maze Estates." She finishes her speech with a sarcastic smile before purposefully walking off. Obviously, she will not be an ally of mine, but she was helpful enough.

As I wander over to the office area, I interrogate my brain in a desperate attempt to remember whether Miranda said to go to the left or right office. I decide to go with the right because, ironically, it feels right. Inside the first office sits a man who looks anemic and appears to be in his mid-thirties. He is vigorously tapping the keys on his computer. I clear my throat to attract his attention. He jumps in his seat, nervously, before looking up and seeing me uncomfortably chilling in the doorway. If I was not so awkward, I would have, ya know, gone in, introduced myself, been a grown up, but they say to be yourself and such mature actions are way too out of character.

The man lurches out of his seat and gets to me in no less than three huge strides. He grabs my left hand with both of his sweaty ones before giving it a shift shake as he says, "hello there, you must be June. I recognize you from the photo you sent with your application… Not that I looked at it an abnormal amount or anything. I mean, I did review your application a couple of times, but that was just to be thorough. I mean, it's just customary you know." He chuckles, anxiously before continuing. "Anyways I'm Michael, uh Michael Lowe. We've emailed a little."

Honestly, my heart goes out to the fella. Not only are his words a little odd, but his voice sounds like his sinuses are permanently infected. Adding to this, he keeps sucking in air as if he is having a lung-collapsing, asthma attack. It is painfully obvious that he is not at ease. I feel sympathetic to this. Our situation is edgy. We know of each other, but do not know each other personally. At least he is being nice. If high school had taught me anything, it was that kindness is a rarity. I will gladly accept awkward over arrogant any day.

"That's me! It's great to put a face to your name! So, I guess this is where I can check in and fill out the extra paperwork and all that fun stuff." I reply. I have a sweet-sounding voice in general, and I propel myself to sound more confident in an attempt to help the man relax. I know my plan is working when I see Michael's shoulders move farther from his ears.

A toothy smile spreads across his face as he retreats back to his desk and begins explaining the process. "Yes, ma'am! I've got your papers in a file, uh somewhere around here. Oh, please set your stuff down and take a seat!"

I stack my things carefully on the floor. I lower into the metal chair that faces him as he slides a pen, resting upon a stack of papers, my way. "There are just a few rules I'm going to need to read to you, and just a few documents for you to sign. When we are done, I'll page Lacey and see if I can get her in here. If not, I'll just take you up to your room. That way, you can get settled in and everything. Bless your heart, I am sure you are ready to put your stuff away. Oh, and you need a tour still. Sorry, there's just so much to do!" Michael explains in a rushed tone. *Yeah, you're telling me.* I am running on four hours of sleep and am incredibly close to curling up into a ball and taking a nap on this thinly-lined carpet.

Here is a summary because the detailed-to-a-tee regulations are far too mundane. Basically, if I talk about a patient's personal thoughts to anyone, ever, or if I give them advice on anything, even if it is merely to blow their nose, I will be up against a firing squad. *Kidding,* but I will get tossed in jail. Plus, Maze will get sued for every quarter, nickel, and penny they are worth, which after seeing the building's outside paint job, I am going to venture into saying is not much. I find the majority of the other rules exceedingly hardcore and unnecessary. I can definitely follow them generally enough to not get in trouble. I plan to play on loop-holes.

Michael finishes describing the limitations fast enough. Soon, he is asking for my signature as if I am doing him the largest of favors. I glide my messy John Hancock across all nine papers. A tsunami of relief washes over me the second the last mark is made.

Within a minute of finishing the paperwork, I

hear a princess-like voice behind me. "Hey, Mike! Are y'all almost done?"

He replies too fast, almost tripping over his words. "Miss Lacey! You have superb timing. We just now finished. It is my pleasure to introduce you to your intern. This here is June Wilson."

When Michael motions to me, I rotate my head to study my new mentor. She is a tad over my height, which is 5.4. She has elbow-length, wavy tow-colored blonde hair and eyes the color of semi-sweet chocolate chips. Her skin is clear, but her facial coloration very uneven. Scattered splotches of red are peeping through the layer of foundation on her face. Her slight plumpness is emphasized by her wide set hips. She is dressed in dusty rose-colored scrubs. This color makes her eyes pop, and her lips look youthfully pink. Overall, she is an attractive woman. I assume the oldest she can be is thirty.

In a way, Lacey looks and strikingly sounds, similar to my late sister, Elizabeth. I attempt to not over-analyze this. I grin sweetly, but timidly, at her. She intimidates me. After all, she is going to basically be my boss for the next eight weeks.

Without missing a beat, Lacey begins talking. "Hi doll face! Oh, my goodness how cute are you with that head of red hair? You are adorable! I have been so excited all day to meet you! I am absolutely honored to help you make the most out of this program. We are going to have a great time!" I am not sure how to respond, so I just keep smiling.

"Well anywho, if you're all set here let me take you upstairs!" She continues. Lacey sounds a little too happy for somebody employed by a mental institution. Guess you must be a little insane to truly enjoy it.

Michael begins bidding farewell, and I sense my nerves inflame with social anxiety at the thought of being alone with Lacey.

"Yep, I believe she's ready! Let me just give you a couple things, June." Michael rummages through his desk drawer. "Here is a map of Maze, in case you get a little lost. The place can be a bit tricky. Here is your name tag. Please, try to remember to wear it whenever you leave your room. They are very helpful to the patients. I think that is it though, you should be all set now. Any questions?" Michael asks while handing me the two items.

"Nope, I think I'm good here. Thanks for everything!" I reply with sincerity.

"Alright then. You enjoy yourself and come to me, or somebody around here, if you need anything. Take care of her Lacey. I think this girl is a good one." Michael says before winking.

Lacey chuckles as she begins helping me gather my luggage. That is the last of the first-level formalities. I am finally traveling to the much-discussed 'upstairs.'

As Lacey and I begin walking, I am finally able to muster some words. "Sorry, I didn't really get to say anything to you a second ago, but I'm so overjoyed to be here. I cannot wait to start working with you!" I tell her in an attempt to sound social.

"Oh hun, you will love it! Maze is a neat experience. We have some of the sweetest patients around." She replies. Her statement is hysterical.

Does she go and interview other mentally insane people around the area? You know, just to make sure Maze is in-fact home to the sweetest? *I highly doubt it.*

Lacey guides me through the den area I saw earlier. Then, we come to a halt at a new-age looking elevator encased within the left wall. The staircase had been concealing it earlier, so my lazy self is grateful to now be aware of a cuttable corner. As we wait for the elevator to get on our level, Lacey babbles away. She continues as we ride up to the third floor and proceed down the longest hallway my eyes have ever seen. She is droning on about where she is from, how she started working here, and about her husband and children. To sum it up, she is talking about herself. Let's be real, everyone, including myself, loves to do just that. We find ourselves the most interesting. It is simply human nature. Still, I cannot get a damn word in.

Lacey abruptly stops speaking as we approach a room labeled 320. I silently wish it was 420 because I'm a tad immature, and still thinking about how nice it was getting high with my favorite brother last week. Lacey fusses with the card she is swiping before finally prying open the door. The fact that the room key is identical to one of a hotel is comical and all too ironic.

"Here you go, girly!" Lacey chirps as she hands the card off to me. "As I am sure Michael told you, staff members get skeleton keys. If lost, it could be detrimental to the facility. So, let's not allow that to happen. Keep it with you at all times and do not let patients see it under any circumstances. I usually place mine in my bra strap, but that may be a tad unkosher. Other people slide it behind their name tag. I'm not real worried about you doing this, but please, please don't use the key to access other people's rooms. This place has cameras, so I promise you will get caught. The door locks automatically, which means you do not have to worry about locking yours. That comes in handy!"

"I completely understand," I respond, absentmindedly.

Honestly, I am a little distracted from her instructions. I am dying to inspect my new room. As promised, I have a double-sized bed facing a small television that is attached to a rather large DVD player. Collecting dust beside the TV is a mini fridge supporting a burnt-out microwave. The bed is framed with a single side-table that rests contently underneath an olive colored lamp. The window opposite to where Lacey and I are standing is small and square, but I can see sky, so it serves its purpose. To the left of the microwave-fridge contraption, is the outline of a shallow closet. On the other side, lies a door that presumably leads to a bathroom. The room houses no flourishes or excitement, but it is not a padded cell which makes it perfectly good enough.

"Here we have your new home away from home! All the appliances should work, though I doubt you'll really use them that much. This is your little powder room here." Lacey explains as she opens the bathroom door swiftly. She closes it before I can even sneak a peek. "And you get it all to yourself! Everything look good to you? Any questions or anything?" She continues, speaking at ninety miles-an-hour. I am disappointed as the grammar police does not show up to pull her over.

"Everything looks just swell!" I reply. *Swell? Really? Now is not the time to experiment with new adjectives, June.*

"Okee dokee. Well, I'm gonna give you an ounce of time to rest that pretty face. I'll be back around say, 7:30ish? The patients go to dinner anytime between 5:30 and 7:00. Then, everyone else goes after in shifts. That should be a good time for us to eat and to let you meet the other interns. Then later, after everyone goes back to their rooms for the night, we'll tour!" Lacey exclaims, again in a single breath.

She may not be letting me wedge in a word, but at least she is honestly making an effort. "Sounds like a plan!" I respond eagerly. I'll admit to being absolutely stoked. Butterflies are swirling around my belly in anxious elation. Consider me officially plucked from my accustomed elements.

For the first time since I turned 18, I feel like a real-life adult. With all these foreign surroundings, I truly am grateful for Lacey's kindness. Her radiating warmth brings me comfort. I appreciate this; it almost makes me feel safe. Well, as safe as one can feel in a literal asylum.

# CHAPTER THREE: FRENZIED

I know I need to unpack. Somehow my new-found freedom evokes a will. Disclaimer: I am not the most organized person to have graced the earth, however being away from home makes me feel a wave of obligation to have a living space that does not resemble a pig-sty. What a wonderful and unforeseen side effect of independence. Maybe being neat will lead to a well-rounded June. I can see the headlines now: *Local girl puts shirts on hangers and underwear in drawers. Becomes instant saint. A miracle thriving amongst us.*

It does seem a bit pointless that I am going through the trouble of unpacking when I am just going to be forced to repeat the process in two months. On top of that, I will only be home for a couple of weeks before moving my clutter to college. This whole concept is downright tedious and a little frustrating. Realizing my heroic act to be in vain, I abruptly halt my unpacking. I let a strapless bra slip through my fingers and back into the suitcase before propelling my body onto the firm, actually rock hard, mattress. I then take this opportunity to avoid adulthood for the next thirty minutes by staring blankly at the ceiling, watching the fan spin as if I am in a trance. Okay, maybe I am not going to be a tidy person. Perhaps I can master cooking, or start reading to the blind, or feed nasty, beady-eyed ducks clumps of stale bread. Yeah, I'll just improve my life with another worthy attribute.

Lacey is a woman of her word. At 7:29, I hear the quick thumping of hyper knocks sounding at my door. By that time, I have changed into the sapphire blue scrubs I bought a couple of weeks prior. They feel like stretchy sandpaper, but unfortunately, they are standard dress code. Lacey beams at me as I almost rip a nail off trying to pry open my heavy door.

Standing a step or two behind Lacey is a wiry girl with long, licorice-colored hair pulled back into a tight bun. Ill-fitting glasses frame her hazel eyes. The green tint to her irises is pretty, but her eyes are startlingly far set on either side of her witch-like nose. Only brief patches of her sallow skin are left untouched by blemishes, and the scars they leave.

I feel a little bad for the girl. She is not gross, but she definitely is not attractive. I have a hunch that she is smart. She resembles a girl who shoved me in kindergarten. At most, she might be a year older than me.

I can almost sense that we will have sub-zero in common. Though the girl is obviously not over the top preppy, something I resent, it is apparent from her bluntly, unamused face that she is most likely a snob. Oh God, possibly even somebody that snorts.

*Wait, I do that. I would like to change my answer to somebody who chews with their mouth open.* But it has been drilled into my head since childhood that you should not judge a book by its cover and what not. I flash a nervous smile at the two.

"June, this is Miss Victoria! She is one of the interns. The only other gal. I'm sure y'all will be the best of friends!" Exclaims an animated Lacey.

*Yeah, I'm sure we will be BFF's. Practically sisters. Kindred spirits even.* "It's great to meet you, Victoria," I say, trying to give the girl a chance.

"Uh yeah, you too." She replies with an uninterested eye roll. My heart immediately brims with disdain, and my lungs become heavy with embarrassment.

All traces of friendliness slip from my face as I coldly ask, "Are we both interning under you, Lacey?"

"Well, Victoria will be with Noelle three days a week and with us for two days! Noelle doesn't work Mondays and Tuesdays, lucky dog. She's been here for literally forever though, so she's earned it. That's why Victoria is with us tonight! We'll have so much fun! I love, love, love getting girl time!" Good Lord, is Lacey really this perky? Her over-the-top demeanor is starting to unhinge my nerves in slight. How do I interact with her? I am soft-spoken and meek as a mouse. Lacey is bold and very expressive.

Victoria glares at Lacey with radiating intensity. I guess I can scrounge up some comfort in that this girl is not in good with Lacey or anything. If those two had been in cahoots, I would have struggled so much more to be... myself? Even if myself is awkward? Like, I would have been too nervous to actually be June-ish.

Lacey's chirpy voice interrupts my thoughts. "Let's grab some dinner ladies!"

If I could use one word to describe the cafeteria it would be, overwhelming. Automatic doors glide open to reveal a massive, slick, grey-colored room. It is larger than my high school gymnasium. Three of the walls are consumed by six different food lines. They all have separate labels including: "Pizza", "Homestyle", "Drinks", "Salad", "Sandwiches" and "Dessert." *I cannot wait for months of pistachio pudding and cold pot roast. What a delight.*

The center of the gigantic room is littered with long rectangular tables. What seems like a million scrub-clothed-people are scarfing down their food, while attempting to make obligated conversation with tolerated co-workers. I know that soon, I will blend into the crowd and be nothing more than one of them.

"Well, here we are! Whatcha ladies in the mood for? They cook up a mean Salisbury steak over at the Homestyle line!" Suggests Lacey.

"I don't eat red meat," Victoria replies flatly. *Personally, I love to consume dead animals.*

I eagerly watch Lacey struggle to react politely. To my surprise, Lacey cocks her head to the side and replies, "just get whatever you will eat and meet us when you're done then" without an ounce of hesitation. My stunned gaze follows Victoria as she stalks over to the salad bar, sullenly. *Crude freak probably drinks unsweet tea.*

"I'm not one to judge, but she ain't too nice. Anyway, what are you wanting to eat, baby doll?" Inquires an offended Lacey.

"Salisbury steak sounds perfect," I reply.

Okay, saying that may have made me bear a resemblance to a teacher's pet but oh well. I need to be close with Lacey. She seems knowledgeable, in a totally gossipy way. I want to be kept in the loop. Maze has to be overflowing with secrets. I bet Lacey knows every last one of them. Plus, like I said, I find deceased, critter-corpse delicious. Salisbury steak used to be one of my favorite meals before my mom gave up cooking and eased into the all-too-popular takeout routine.

Lacey and I journey through the homestyle line together to receive our questionable food from women who are most likely biker gang members. Their facial hair keeping them from being ideal nutrition providers. After we swipe our name tags through this little machine at the end of the line, we venture out into the abyss of tables.

Lacey casually sets her tray down next to a male nurse. He is probably around her age, early thirties. Good looking in the traditional standard of beauty sense. His sleek hair and scruffy beard are black as coal making his aquamarine colored eyes pop against his pale skin. The man smiles pleasantly at Lacey and I as we take a seat. Across from him sits a, and excuse my girliness, dreamy, yet slightly nerdy, teenage guy. Though tall, he has a little too much muscle mass to be considered lanky. His brown-flecked, blonde hair is short, yet a tad fluffy, giving it a laid-back look. The guy's eyes are dark green. They remind me of the seaweed that clings to your ankles the moment you wade into the ocean's salty waves. The color sparkles against his clear, sun-kissed complexion. *Control yourself, June.*

Okay, obviously, I am extremely attracted to him. A wide, crooked smile eats up his face the moment he meets my intrigued gaze revealing that, perhaps, he too is interested in me. He could also just be looking at the gravy stain on my chest from when I attempted to pick up my meat and dropped the tongs a few minutes ago. *The clatter had made me want to gouge my eyes out.*

"Well hey there Lacey! This your intern?" Asks the older of the two gentlemen as he motions toward me.

"It sure is! Boys, this is Miss June Wilson. June this is Pierce. He might just be the best RN we've got, and this is…...Oops, I'm drawing a complete blank. I'm so sorry darlin.' I know they have told me your name, but remind me real quick?" Lacey asks sheepishly. She turns to my future husband, a look of embarrassment blatant on her round face.

He chuckles before replying. "Oh no problem, I'm Evan. It's nice to meet you guys." He extends his long arm and gives her hand a firm shake before doing the same to mine.

From the moment he speaks, I can tell he is not from around here. His accent sounds midwestern. I become a little apprehensive, scared he may be a cold yankee. Turns out, I am just being a hair judgmental. *Imagine that.* Of course, everyone gives the customary "great to meet you" before beginning to eat.

I have just bitten into my first fork-full of tough, overcooked beef when Victoria startles me by slamming her tray down next to mine. Crazy girl almost knocks over my lemon-accented sweet tea. *You just don't do that.*

"All the food here looks repulsive. I've already lost my appetite for the summer." She proclaims in the most entitled of tones.

"Victoria this is Pierce and his intern Evan. Um, this is Victoria. She's not quite settled in yet." Lacey offers, attempting to compensate for Victoria's ridiculous behavior. I can tell Victoria is on the brink of shooting a pissy remark at Lacey but is frozen in her tracks when she faces forward. Her eyes landing on Evan.

It is almost as if Victoria is trying to show us a preview of bipolar disorder. Her face brightens immediately, like a damn ray of sunshine. She attempts to flip her hair in flirtation before awkwardly realizing it is trapped in a mess of bobby pins. She reaches across me and holds her visibly clammy hand open to Evan.

"You can call me Tori if you want. It's so nice to meet the final intern." She says in a sugary tone as he accepts her shake, a look of reluctance in his eyes.

"Very nice to meet you as well, Victoria." Okay, I do not think his reply had to be that polite. I feel a twinge of jealousy working its way into my system.

In high school, I constantly got walked on by other girls. It is a wonder I did not get trampled to death. It was not necessarily because they were prettier than me, it was correlated more to their personalities. I always lost guys to confident, loud, and goofy girls. I am apparently too shy and "complicated." However, I will never apologize for having depth. This is why Victoria makes me feel insecure. I hope this Evan guy is intelligent enough to realize her dull appearance matches her fake persona.

"So y'all, I want everybody to get to know each other! It'll make workin' smoother if we know more about our people, don't y'all think?! Evan, you start. Give us a little run-down on yourself!" Lacey encourages, trying her hardest to strike a conversation. Hey, she gets an A for effort.

Evan does not oppose. He gladly volunteers some facts. "Sure thing! I'm Evan Carter. I'm from a town called Avon up in Colorado." *Oops, drop the mid. I guess it's just western.* "My parents work for a ski resort a little south of there. I've been a competitive skier since I was seven. So, I guess you could say I was pretty involved in the resort too, but not anymore! I just graduated high school, and I am stoked to be going to Colorado State this fall. I'm here in 'Bama because my mom is from Huntsville.

Her uncle was actually checked into Maze towards the end of his life. He died this past summer, and I met one of last year's interns here when we came down for the funeral. They told me all about the program and, since I want to be a sociologist, it sounded like a good fit for me. I applied, and well here I am. On a more personal note, I love seafood, my Siamese cat named Jason is my best pal, and my favorite movie is *Demolition Man*." He finishes his spill with a cheeky grin. To my surprise and delight, he turns to me. "What's your story?"

I feel my cheeks flush with scarlet color. Delight quickly morphs into dread. Oh man, is my voice going to tremble, perhaps even crack. I fear being put on the spot like the plague. Honestly, I think I would prefer the black buboes and imminent death over the volunteering of fun facts.

I inhale deeply and attempt a relaxed-looking smile before replying. "Um, I'm June. Oh, I guess you already know that. I'm the second to youngest of a big family. I have two sisters and one brother. So, I needed to get away, try to find my own identity. Wow, that sounds kinda sad to say out loud. I mean I have an identity--" *Going downhill fast, June.*

"Uh anyway, that is what led me to Maze. I only live a few hours away. I'm 18, I just graduated, and I'll be going to Auburn in a few months. Uh, go tigers! I too love cats. I have two. I have an ongoing affair with movies, that don't suck, and sleep. Those are basically my hobbies. I'm a little shy, so it may take me a while to get comfortable with all of you guys. Don't give up on me though! Um, that's kind of it I guess." Could my dialogue be more saturated with social awkwardness? At least I tried. That counts for something, right? Oh yeah, and I did not accidentally say two sisters.

Victoria sighs as an effort to pull attention to herself. We all look over at her in annoyance. "Okay, I'll keep it short. I'm Victoria Burns. I'm from Valdosta, that's in Georgia. I graduated top of my class last year, and now I go to UGA. I'm a psych major, so I went looking for internships that dealt with anything mental. My advisor found this one, it seemed close, sounded decently impressive and now I'm here, obviously. I enjoy playing tennis, I read poetry often, and-" she bats her makeup-free eyelashes at Evan before finishing her sentence, "am a very fun, easy to talk to kind of girl." I, along with Lacey and Pierce, immediately cringe.

I feel Evan gently kick me under the table. I try to gather enough strength to not only stifle a laugh but to also conceal my relief. Not only is he not falling for her ridiculousness, but he is even trying to connect with me.

Lacey, Pierce, Evan, and I make light conversation for the remainder of that night's dinner. Victoria only speaks when Evan speaks and scowls at the rest of us.

The guys finish their meals a few minutes before us girls. They promise to meet us at 10:00 PM in the foyer to start the tour, before excusing themselves. The moment the pair exit earshot, Victoria turns to me.

"Back off, sweetheart, I call him. He was clearly interested in me and obviously did not appreciate you fawning all over him." She loudly instructs. Every fiber of my being urges me to slap her hard enough to loosen a whack tooth from her metal braces. I refrain. I will be like the great Martin Luther King Jr. and avoid violence. I do, however, consider backing over her with my car when leaving Maze. *I'm sure I could make that look*

34

*like an accident.*

Lacey does not approve of her saying this to me, to say the very least. "Victoria, dear, I'm going to be real blunt with you. If you don't change that attitude of yours, I will personally make sure you do not stay in this program. This internship is a privilege. You are going to be respectful to everyone you have the pleasure of meeting here, or you are going to have to explain to your parents why Maze, which is in Alabama, sent you back home to Valdosta."

Wow, I am beyond impressed with Lacey. She is one tough cookie. Plus, she is not even finished yet. "I could care less what y'all do with Evan. That ain't any of my business, but for the record, he was not looking at you with affection. Why would he? You were being rude and hateful from the moment you sat down. No guy finds that attractive. So, shape up. Am I making myself clear?"

Victoria shrugs. She stares at the tile floor before murmuring a barely audible, "yes ma'am."

I cannot tell how this dynamic with Victoria is going to affect the summer for me. I know she does not possess the ability to spoil my experience. However, an uncomfortable tension will always be present whenever I am forced to share air with the bitchy gal.

This is the first time I realize the obvious. I struggle to swallow a dry lump in my suddenly itchy throat as the thought crashes into me. I may have graduated high school, but I will never leave. College, work, and social settings will forever reflect a juvenile dynamic in some aspect. All I can do is hope to be fortunate enough to find a decent group. I would have breezed through high school if I could have tolerated just a handful of people. Hopefully, I'll be luckier from now on.

Victoria's response satisfies Lacey. She straightens her shoulders and alters her face to display positivity. "Alrighty, so here's the game plan ladies, I've got some patients to check on. So y'all are gonna go back to your rooms for a few hours. You are not meeting any patients till tomorrow. Don't worry, like I said, I'll come to get y'all for touring around 10:00! Y'all remember where your rooms are?" asks Lacey.

Victoria and I quickly nod yes. "Okay well y'all head on back! Go straight there. I don't want any mischief ladies!" Lacey orders.

I walk back to the elevator feeling a little disappointed. I am restless and ready to get rolling. *Bring on the crazies*. I know I will, most likely, be dying for some downtime in the future. Sadly, you cannot will yourself to think a certain way. I think people would be a lot happier if they could realize that. Maybe I should not say happier, but more at peace.

# CHAPTER FOUR: SCREWY

I am proud to successfully end up in the correct room. I am perpetually on the challenged side when it comes to navigation. Once in, I plop down on my soft comforter and switch on the TV. I see a Jack icicle being forced into arctic waters by a teary-eyed Rose. Great, the movie that is an anti-ad for cruises is playing.

Honestly, I have conflicting views about this groundbreakingly-popular film. I find it to be completely unrealistic. Nobody becomes so engrossed with irrevocable love in three days. If, the characters even knew each other that long, *Absolutely preposterous*. I guess, if I want to be realistic, the ship only sailed for a few days. Some exaggeration is necessary for the plot. I will admit, I do enjoy watching it when I need to release some waterworks. I try not to feel too much during my daily routine. By default, I need to force some emotion out. Miserable movies seem to help.

When I need an outlet, I prefer to watch movies

that are upsetting from beginning to end. Movies purely plotted by tragedy. Usually, one where a child is killed. I know how that sounds, but child death is horrifying. Any movie that kills off a kid leaves the audience disturbed. Even if the plot is underdeveloped or acted out badly, it mesmerizes viewers with heart-ache. It is like an itchy feeling; an itch you can't scratch because it has infested into your emotions. That is the part of this movie that actually gets to me. The part where the third-class mother is tucking her children into bed, even though the ship is being overthrown by the ocean. The deeply-ingrained pain plaguing the mother's eyes is almost authentic.

I am not assuming that the woman is a mediocre actress. *I am not that cynical.* I have just been exposed to the facial expression first hand. My own mother held that softly-agonized gaze in her saltwater-overwhelmed eyes when my sister died. It was not the look I saw when my parents first processed Elizabeth's death. I did not see it as my mother was looking down at Lizzie's motionless body, nestled in white satin and posed in an unnaturally calm position. She was not even wearing that face as they lowered her daughter into the cold, uninviting ground for all of eternity. It was when she turned to us that I witnessed the strange hurt infiltrate her eyes.

She gaped at me and my remaining siblings as we sat around Lizzie's grave site. I guess you could call them front row seats, but I always refer to them as the true electric chairs. Once I caught a full blast of my mother's tortured stare, I turned away sharply and attempted to find a distraction.

I did not fully understand the look until a few months later. The same movie I am watching now was playing on cable. I saw the distinct sentiment in the mother's eyes as she bid her doomed children goodnight, and I resonated with the emotion. Suddenly, I had the realization of what was going through my own mother's mind the day of Lizzie's funeral, raging fear. She had come to the horrifying conclusion that her children were truly mortal. She could not protect us from everything. Death is inevitable. She is simply human, and so are we. The knowledge that your children could perish before you is terrifying. No matter what my relationship with my mom may be, the thought of her being forced to process the unimaginable makes me feel winded.

Yeah, I flip that damn channel. I feel a surge of relief course through my veins as the eerie theme song of *The X-Files* fills my petite room. My heart swelters with adoration for this show. I have an irrational crush on Agent Mulder. His accentuated nose equals perfection, and I am instantly calmed by the image of his familiar face playing across the screen.

A loud bang startles my door, causing me to gasp and jump as if I am experiencing the beginning effects of a grand mal seizure.

Perhaps, and I could be wrong about this, watching a couple episodes of *The X-Files* while in an asylum is not the epitome of bright ideas. It's just, if I want to see some incestuous hicks get abducted by aliens, ain't nobody going to stop me.

"Uh, come in?" I mumble, hesitantly. I hear the swipe of a key and immediately relax when I see Evan's outline slip through my door.

The rush of relief is short-lived. I am suddenly overcome with a mixture of confusion and embarrassment. *What time is it? Was he supposed to come get me? I look like a homeless man on crack who has just finished eating a can of Fancy Feast.*

I clear phlegm from my throat and attempt a smile as I let go of the pillow I have unintentionally clutched. *He's cute, but he is an intruder.*

Evan approaches my bed slowly, grinning in amusement. "Sorry didn't mean to scare ya. Lacey asked Pierce to call me and say to grab you guys and come downstairs. I wanted to get you first because that other chick kind of gives me the creeps." He finishes his explanation with a wink.

"Uh yeah. She's kind of impossible to like, but hey at least we have each other! Just let me throw on shoes, and we can go." Wow, I am surprised by both my flirtatious statement and easy tone. Perhaps, independence is affecting me nicely.

"X-files, huh? Retro girl. Probably still scarier than any new-age horror trash." Evan comments while plopping down on my bed.

"Totally. The storylines are never off-point. If only someone would kill off Agent Scully. Such a whiner, you know?" I reply.

He whips back a response without an ounce of hesitation. "Hell no! Scully and Mulder are the couple. He would be nowhere without her lab skills."

"Uh, they aren't even together. Whatever, agree to disagree." I say with an attempt at a wink. More like a face seizure, *great.*

"Okay, let's get this party started." I murmur sarcastically to Evan as he gets up to open my door.

As we wander over to Victoria's room, the conflict of who would summon the goblin arises.

"You knock," Evan begs.

"No way in hell," I reply.

"C'mon pretty please?" The shmuck is not relenting.

"No, you're the guy, be a man," I argue.

"Exactly, I'm a dude. Y'all have the whole girl bond going on." *By bond do you mean desire to suffocate with a pillow?*

"Oh, my goodness, fine. You are such a baby." I finally succumb to his pleading, emerald eyes. My hand trembles as it places the gentlest of raps on Victoria's door. Our brief flirtation pleased me to a pathetic point.

The thing is, I am only as much of myself as my social anxiety will let me be, and our teasing was adorable. After a couple of seconds, I hear a stir. Then a fleet of solid stomps approach the door. It pops open, my heart rate increases nervously. I succumb to a giggle when the big, bad monster is revealed. Victoria is standing there in nothing but a baggy cotton sweatshirt and female briefs. Her ratty hair is infected with a severe case of bedhead. Her rheum-encrusted eyes are bloodshot and annoyed. Obviously, somebody had not remembered that bedtime was not yet upon us.

Evan cowers behind me, making it my

responsibility to address the peeved girl. "We're supposed to tour tonight, remember?"

"I'll get to it tomorrow. Thanks." Victoria says as she slams her door on us, causing the frame to shake.

I shift my gaze towards Evan. We share a simultaneous shrug. This is how I presume Victoria will act for the remainder of the summer. She will only do what she wants. Nobody will change that. In a twisted way, I admire her will. I let myself be swayed far too often. Sometimes, though, being agreeable is necessary. Everyone's apparent dislike of Victoria is a testimony of that concept.

As we stroll over to the elevator, Evan effortlessly buzzes with chatter. He goes on about his parents, and how they freaked out over his departure. Honestly, I am not paying an abundance of attention. My mind is saturated with dread when it comes to this aspect of getting to know somebody. Sounds mean, but it is the truth. I hate to hear people talk about their families because, nine times out of ten, it means they are on the verge of asking about mine.

"So, must have been nice growing up with a big family! Always someone to play with all the time. That kind of stuff." Well, look at that. *How ironic.*

"It was fun, sometimes. I mean it had good and bad. Kinda like every family, I guess." I reply, flatly with an indifferent half-smile. Per my good fortune, the elevator doors split at that exact moment to reveal Lacey and Pierce standing on the main level. Their eyes widen with surprise as they realize we are a pair, not a trio.

We tell them the spiel about Victoria's disobedience. Lacey lets out a frustrated groan before saying in an aggravated, and thick, southern accent, "I just don't know what I'm going to do with that little lady. I may have to get the girl re-evaluated. She can't act like such an entitled brat in front of the patients!"

Evan and I tense in astonishment and awkwardness. *Did she really say that in front of us?* Pierce shoots Lacey a "hey shut up and be professional or your ass is getting fired" glance. I feel Evan secretly tap my arm. I immediately understand that he is trying to let me know we have mutual feelings regarding the situation. *We are basically engaged.*

I suppress the chuckle his gesture produces, just in time for Lacey to gather her wits. Her already rosy cheeks fade from flushed scarlet back to normalcy. Her features soften like left-out butter.

"Sorry y'all. I don't know what has gotten into me these days. Think I need the tiniest bit of an attitude adjustment." Lacey laughs gratuitously hard at herself after admitting this. "I'm sure Victoria is a fantastic person. We are just having a sort of misunderstanding. Don't you worry though, I'm gonna get it all ironed out! Let's get this tour a goin', shall we?" I like Lacey, and if she wants to bash Victoria then it is fine by me. *We can even do it with a bat.*

I'm going to summarize the tour because, to be blunt, it is grossly boring. Really, the facility is irrelevant to the grand scheme of this experience.

Highlights: movie and craft rooms on the third floor along with the library and staff rooms. Psych offices on fifth, resting areas on main, and patient rooms on second. Visitors are only allowed in the central foyer. My hope is that the institution turns out to be haunted, so my summer may involve a paranormal immersion. Oh! Or maybe the asylum will burn down, fall apart, or become disease-ridden while I am here. *I'm not picky, whatever keeps things interesting.*

Apparently, we are going to engage in weekly outings on a big charter bus. According to Lacey, it has the words "Maze Estates" printed all over it. *Like advertisement.* I, along with the other interns, may go on as many of these so-called adventure days as my little heart desires. We are all required to attend at least one a week. For the most part, the interns can go to town as much as they wish. Obviously, we cannot miss large chunks of the day or week, but we are allowed to run and get stuff or go out to dinner. We need to be back before 10:30 PM, or we will be locked out. If that happens, we are welcome to sleep in our cars. *What a treat.*

The most interesting part of the tour is the fourth level. This is called the treatment floor. This is where the pharmacy along with the small emergency rooms are. On the far-left side, terminally ill patients are attended to. Lacey warns us that they are the worst. The most pitiful, the most pleading, the most delusional. We will not be around them.

This internship has strict guidelines and regulations in terms of who we may play with; I mean observe. Only high functioning patients, who have been dubbed as incapable of harm, are eligible for involvement. Still, even most of them did not consent to being around us. We end up having just a handful of assigned patients. That will work to my advantage though, makes personal connections much easier to obtain. On the far-right side of the fourth floor, is the shock room. Yep, the shock therapy room. That's still a living institution, corrupt as it may be. We are ordered to never even attempt to get in there. It is indefinitely off-limits.

"Okay, sweet peas! That's Maze for y'all. Any questions?" Lacey asks as we ride the elevator back to the third floor. Evan and I shake our heads no in one fluent motion.

"Alrighty! June I'll come to get you at 8 AM sharp, so get some rest!" She continues as the machine screeches to a shaky stop.

"Same for you, Evan," Pierce grumbles, his tone husky with exhaustion. We give the two nurses the mandatory okays and goodnights before they resume their stance in the elevator and head back to their real homes that house their actual families.

The concept of our mentors not actually living at Maze 24/7 is intimidating. Of course, I know they cannot be expected to stay on account of us, but still, l would have felt more comfortable knowing they were around. I guess if I refrain from trouble, I will not need Lacey during the night. Surely nothing bad is actually going to happen. This is not a movie. A patient is most likely not on the verge of a homicidal rampage. I will not wake up to a schizo sawing my throat with a plastic knife. I just need to stay calm and remember, I am most likely in zero danger.

Evan and I roam back to our rooms in radio silence. We are both tired and overwhelmed. Maze is a maze. I am going to get confused and make mistakes, and so is he. That realization seems to sink into us as we approach our opposing doors in a zombie resembling haze. Evan summons a miniscule surge of energy once we reach our parting point. I think he feels guilty for not speaking to me and is trying to compensate with his farewell for the night.

"Let's keep each other sane, Juney. Sound like a plan?" Evan asks with a cat-like yawn and subdued grin.

"Sounds perfect, Evan," I say, smoothly. *You go girl.*

"Night then." He bids.

"Goodnight," I reply with an embarrassingly large smile that seems to say I want to lose my virginity to you.

I shove open my door and enter my still unfamiliar room. I proceed straight to the bathroom without an ounce of reluctance. I peel off my scrubs and step into a steaming shower. Showers are indescribable. You procrastinate taking them, deem it a hassle. But once you succumb to standing beneath the heated water, you realize the depth of its pleasure. I prefer showering in the dark. I find it serene and secure. I love the feeling of having no light shining down, penetrating me with judgment. My eyes are blocked from seeing flaws, my sense of sight on mute. I can only feel.

Once I am dry, well dry-ish because I am critically impatient. I step into my favorite cream lace underwear. The garment is ratted with holes and tattered with fray, but hey they are soft. Then I pull one of my brother's high school football shirts over my damp hair. I love sleeping in guys t-shirts. They are so much roomier than women's. Since I have never obtained a serious boyfriend, I stole a handful of Jamie's shirts before he left for his first tour.

I crawl into the never-before-used cotton sheets and flip on the fan I have placed on my bedside table. I have a strange issue with heat. I sleep with a fan blowing in my face, even in the dead of winter. I am obsessed with being so cold that I must snuggle into a ball under my blankets to keep warm.

As I lay in my empty bed and begin to seek out sleep, I feel like I did when I was a little girl growing. I would get too scared to make it to the morning portion of sleepovers at friends' houses. My mother, or Addison, would typically have to pick me up. I was not scared of demons or phantoms. I just had a feeling. A feeling of impending dread. That if I was not with my family, something awful would happen to them. Like a bomb would explode if I was not there to stop it. I know it's an irrational concept, but I could never get past that idea. The fear would not ease until I was back home and usually sleeping next to one of my siblings. That is exactly how I feel tonight. Instead of being the eighteen-year-old I am, and forcing the thoughts and emotions away, I sob myself into a shallow slumber. *Like a real adult.*

# CHAPTER FIVE: NUTTY

I feel dazed when I awake the following morning at 7:10. Fresh drool is seeping from the corner of my mouth. My mind is still hazily attached to the dream I have abruptly been yanked from. I can vaguely recall the image of me and the cookie monster in a heated brawl over a broken necklace made of snickerdoodles. Peculiar, that dreams only make sense when you are within them. I wonder if our reality only makes sense while we are here. If there is an afterlife, maybe we will arrive there and be overrun with clarity. Like our earthly being is just another blurred level of our subconscious.

*You must get up, June.* Deep down, I am aware that I withhold the power to force myself into a sitting position. I am fighting that power, mentally restraining my body from being physically active. Sleep is an addictive drug. It lures me back into its strong clutches. I close my lethargic eyes for what seems like eight seconds, but in fact, is twenty freaking minutes. I hold my bedside clock up, and then chuck it in disbelief as it reads 7:30.

*Away to the bathroom I flew like a flash.* I cannot decide whether to chuckle or shriek in terror when I see my mess of a reflection in the mirror. I slumped into bed before my hair dried. The result is a tangled catastrophe of copper-colored curls. I definitely do not have time to straighten it. I rake my thick locks back into a loose bun and curl my bangs with a hot iron in an attempt to still look feminine. Then I put on my face. That expression makes me think of Ed Gein and giggle. My eyeliner is smudged and my rouge a tad smeared, but I am presentable. I throw on the semi-wrinkled scrubs that I cast to the floor last night and begin a search for footwear. Finally, I locate my shiny white shoes. The jerks were hiding under the bed. I am tying the last lace on these dirt seeking missiles when I hear a firm knock.

I answer the door to see Lacey beaming at me. "Good morning sunshine! Let's get going we have got a big day!" *Oh God, no.* Lacey is a morning person.

I am sure you cannot imagine this, as I am such a positive gal, but I am far from being an early bird. *Fun fact: mornings are kind of the bane of my existence.* Still, I force a superficial smile, and trail along behind her to the cafeteria like an eager duckling. After pretending to eat the biscuits and gravy Lacey insisted I try, she announces it is time to "get to business."

Finally! *FINALLY.* The reason I am within these crazy walls. It is time to meet some psychos! Um patients, I mean patients. Count this as one of the most crucial days in my life. I would say defining but this day is not going to change me. It is the experience that will.

We, the interns, only focus on the patients, under our mentor's care, who have consented. As I pointed out earlier, few did. Four of the patients that Lacey, Pierce, and Noelle shared were assigned to us.

A startling amount of freedom is allowed at Maze. Like in our country, freedom is fundamental at this institution. The patients that are healthy and, to be blunt, safe enough to wonder their designated areas are welcome to do so. The primary goal is for the mentally unstable to still have a sense of control. I strongly admire the concept. The execution, however, I am weary of.

Overall, it sounds like I will get a good chunk of time with each patient, but keep in mind, they have absolutely no obligation to speak to me. Still, I will get to learn the foundation of what makes them incapable of being... well, actually free.

The first patient I meet is named Pearl. As I hesitantly tiptoe behind Lacey into our designated meeting area, my stomach churns with gushing discomfort. Pearl stares at me as if I am edible. They all do, or at least in my head they do. In reality, I am a naïve and intimidated 18-year-old immersed in a sea of not only strangers but clinically insane ones at that. Once I see Pearl's glazed gaze, I must push remembrance into my mind that this experience is going to be beneficial. *Hopefully.*

Meeting the first patient is the initial step

towards a more knowledgeable future. I force myself to put my foot inside the chilly, perfectly square room and greet the grinning woman with confidence. Or a façade of it. I imagine myself appearing calm and collected, but I'm sure I am actually a muddle of insecurity, and perhaps blatant fear, which could be deemed insulting.

On the way to meet Pearl, Lacey had told me a synopsis of her story. In her prime, Pearl was a blonde bombshell. She worked her magic as a showgirl in Vegas well into her thirties. When she was 41, she had her big break. Unfortunately, it landed her in Maze, not Hollywood.

Apparently, on a freezing morning in February, Pearl stayed in her bathroom from 8:00 AM to 1:00 PM. Her youthful hubby, she was quite the cougar it seems, knocked repeatedly at the door, begging her to let him in. He received no answer. At first, he thought nothing of it. He imagined she was upset over some dispute they had engaged in, ages ago. Pearl was known to hold grudges.

After three consecutive hours of silence, Pearl's husband became fervently concerned. Terrified she had overdosed on cocaine or was violently ill from downing too much sherry the night before, he broke down the door. At first glance, he thought his eyes were deceiving him. His beloved wife was perched on her plush stool facing her vanity. She stared blankly at her reflection with ghastly eyes. A tube of burgundy lipstick was being swirled into her honey-colored locks. All she was wearing was a scarlet-red string bikini and an old pair of Nike Shox. When he asked what she was doing she replied, "being."

Pearl's husband forced a valium down her throat and prayed she would sleep off whatever this funk was. That night she woke up flailing and screeching at the top of her lungs. She claimed to be drowning in air. He rushed her to the emergency room thinking, maybe even hoping, that his wife had hit her head or even had a brain tumor impairing her thought patterns. The doctors could not find a single physical ailment. Eventually, Pearl was diagnosed with a personality disorder as well as chronic depression.

After only six weeks on an antidepressant cocktail, Pearl was dubbed incapable of functioning. Her poor husband was at a total loss. This facility had been recommended to him by several doctors in Nevada. They insisted that getting her away from the life she had known would be beneficial. He took their advice and checked Pearl into Maze. That was six years ago.

As I stretch out an arm to shake Pearl's dainty hand, I am caught off guard by how okay she seems. She makes eye contact, nods, and tells me she is, "delighted to meet my acquaintance." I begin chatting with her and, though I can see her being a little arrogant and delusional, it is hard to imagine insane.

*Again, naïve 18-year-old.* After talking to Pearl for maybe forty minutes or so, she abruptly halts her speech. She simply stares at me, wearing a toothy grin. A few minutes later, and her expression remains stationary. I try to ask her some questions, attempt to find something to spark her back into reality. This is when I notice Lacey has begun to tug on my elbow.

Lacey slices the silence by saying, "we will be seeing you later, Miss Pearl." She then stands up and starts backing away from the window sill Pearl rests on. I swiftly follow. The same smile gleams on Pearl's face as we scurry out. It is almost as if she is a statue or, more accurately, a gargoyle. Frozen in a permanent position. Her creepy expression makes my skin crawl with invisible bugs. Her beam is simply unnatural.

After meeting Pearl, I am ready for a breather. Lacey seems to execute telepathy. She suggests I grab a snack, chill out for an hour, or so. Then meet her in the crafts room so she may introduce me to the next patient.

I skip towards the cafeteria, unfortunately bumping into Victoria on the way. "Have you met Glinda?" She asks.

"Nope," I reply, apprehensively.

"She adores me already. We are getting along famously. I don't know how she's going to feel about you though." Victoria says smugly. Is this really necessary?

For some reason, I indulge her. "Why not?"

Victoria is more than happy to provide an answer. "Well, you've got that awkwardness to you. I mean no offense. It's just that I am sure she can tell when somebody is being fake. I don't think she'll take very well to you being shy. She will think you are hiding something. Won't trust you with a thing." I hate her. I absolutely despise this imp.

"Gotcha," I say flatly to Victoria before turning on my heels and walking the other way.

"Are you not going to the cafeteria, June?" I hear her call out. I do not answer. I am mortified to have not been able to stand up for myself. I just want to go back to my room and be as *awkward* as I want.

Once I barge through my door, I pull out a pack of granola I brought with me to Maze. I begin tearing the stubborn seal before realizing my appetite has been completely compromised. I plop down on the bed, turn my timer for 45 minutes and fall asleep. My mind is so foggy when I return to consciousness, that I almost think I have come down with the crazy, but no, I guess it is not airborne. I lay in the midst of blankets for a few minutes too long before realizing I am supposed to be meeting Lacey at this precise moment.

I grab the half-opened granola from my bedside table and start pouring the honey-coated oats into my hungry mouth as I slip on my shoes. I sprint down the hall, and then the stairs until I find myself in a large, open room with lots of windows and easels. *Windows seems like a hazard.* There are stations for macaroni art, quilting, pottery, and, of course, drawing. My curious eyes scan the room to find Lacey, but she is not amongst the artsy patients. Thank goodness, she is running late also.

My attention is caught by the most beautiful portrait of snow I have ever seen up close. A good-looking man with red hair and fair skin is painting an icy forest with ease. The gentle strokes of his brush effortlessly fabricating the picturesque scene.

I stop munching the granola still in my mouth, as I become engrossed in watching this man work. He seems to feel my burning stare because after a few moments he asks, "have you ever been to Vermont?"

I stammer as I tell him no. He looks over his shoulder at me and grins. "Don't, the maple syrup gave me food poisoning." He chuckles softly. "The snow there is exquisite, though. Let's be real, any snow is when you live in southern Alabama. New nurse or intern?"

"Intern." I pull a stool up next to him.

"I could kind of tell. No offense but you look a little…frightened. I mean why would you be, you're with such grounded people." He says jokingly. *Why is no offense such a popular phrase today?*

I cannot refrain from giggling at his statement. He looks relieved as my face starts to relax. I like this guy. If I did not see the neon orange band around his wrist, I would have guessed he was a worker using his break to paint and not a patient. I quickly become worried that I may have offended him.

"I'm sorry! It's not that I'm scared. This sounds lame, but I'm kind of on the timid side, and by kind of I mean I have said about three sentences since I've gotten here. Probably not the best thing to admit to people I want to respect me, right?" I tell him in a tone saturated with honesty.

I had said the truth, and it would have been embarrassing if the guy had reacted any differently. He looks me straight in the eye. "Well thank God. Conversation comes hardest to the best people."

"June!" Lacey's high-pitched voice sounds behind me before I can respond to him. She places a set of acrylic nailed fingers on the small of my back and continues. "I see you've met Mr. Creed! He's my sweetie.

"Randall this here is my intern, June. We are supposed to go see Tom right now, but we will be by to visit with you while you are having your morning coffee tomorrow, and, if you both are ready, she may even sit in on your afternoon session tomorrow! How about that?" Well dang. Lacey is the queen of breaking the ice, it is like her pond never even freezes.

"Sounds perfect Lacey. Real nice to meet you, June." Randall replies with a sincere smile and a nod of the head.

I tell him the same, return my stool, and follow Lacey to the opposite side of the room. As we walk, she talks over her shoulder. "Randall is a super nice guy. Quiet, but nice. Between us, I can see him getting out of here before anyone else. I mean the kid is only 27. He just needs to get his chemicals straightened out." Her statement intrigues my attention. I become excited at the prospect of chatting with him more tomorrow.

Before I can interject input on what Lacey has said, she drags me to the corner of the room by the sleeve of my scrub top. She begins bracing me for the next patient we will be meeting, Thomas.

"Okay June, Thomas is complicated. Cheerful guy, but here's the thing. When he was in his early thirties a huge SUV t-boned his convertible BMW. The driver who caused the crash was stopped at a red light. He was on the phone just bickering, having it out with his wife. The guy was so distracted, thought he was getting divorced. The kid beside him, some teenager, thought it was sooo hilarious to push on his gas pedal a little bit and see if it would make the person next to him think the light is green, and run it. They call it chicken or something." I almost have to stop Lacey because that is not at all what playing chicken is.

I know because two kids I went to school with were killed playing chicken on railroad tracks. But it would have been the most know it all thing to do in the history of things done by people who think they know all. Nonetheless, the point is that it was a cruel joke.

"Well, unfortunately, the game worked...Partially. The man on the phone drove his SUV full force into the road, except he did not make it through the light. Tom's car got in the way." Lacey's voice is thickening with emotion. This situation is obviously serious. "The guy in the SUV, he just walked away with bruises. Tom though, poor Thomas, he suffered a severe head trauma. I mean he barely lived through surgery. He came out with substantial brain damage.

"So, now his mind does not process emotions correctly. Like I'll be having a perfectly normal conversation with him about perhaps, sports. I'll say, 'hey Tom catch the Lakers game?' and he will answer yes. He'll start telling me how the ref made bullshit calls. Then he will be like, 'Lacey, I want to blow your fucking head off with a double-barrel shotgun." *Well... That escalated quickly.*

"Or he will break down in hysterics, or start whispering and looking around in paranoia, freaky stuff. You just have to keep a level head with him, June. He will throw you off guard. He is not violent though. I promise hun, he is not going to actually harm you. The worst he has done is hide. Tom has hidden a lot since he's gotten here. It can actually be a bit comical from time to time. One time we found him in the cafeteria freezer eating only the raspberry out of a carton of rainbow sherbet." Lacey informs me, now all smiles. Though he does sound like quite the delightful trickster, I feel incredibly apprehensive about meeting him. What she is telling me is a colossal amount of information to process. *Hey, guess this is what I signed up for.*

Thomas is sitting at a table, laughing and making papier mache swans with himself. Lacey gently guides him over to a set of four bean bags. We three sit and talk for a half hour. Once he starts speaking, a tsunami of sadness washes over me.

I want to go off and weep after the first five minutes of talking to Tom. As horrid as this may make me sound, I think about all the bad people I know. Teachers who despise children, classmates who bully peers, even just people who are condescending to waitresses. If somebody had to be in an accident, I would rather it be a hateful person than somebody as sweet as Thomas.

Then my thoughts diverge. I start considering the fact that when you hear a tragic story, the victim is unfailingly described as loving, or strong, or loyal. People who knew them claim that if there is a heaven, that person is undoubtedly there, living it up. I know I am just digging at the unanswerable question, *why do bad things happen to good people?* But do bad things truly happen to good people? No matter the circumstances, victims are rarely, almost never, described as being conceded, or unfair, or hostile. They are never declared to be Hell-bound.

The thing is though, some have to be. It is simple logic. Perhaps, we are convinced that bad things happen to good people because when something bad happens to a person, they are dubbed good. It's possible that Thomas may have been vile in the past and is only kind currently because of his humbling circumstances. Maybe the bad made him good.

I know this should be consoling because it means there is always a positive thing to be said about any type of person. Is this honestly reassuring though, or is it a form of corruption?

"June...June dear, wasn't it nice to meet Thomas?" Lacey asks, dragging me back to reality. The increased width of her eyes serves as evidence that my disconnect has been obvious, and I am missing my cue to bid a polite farewell.

"Sorry! Yes, Thomas, it was a pleasure." I answer hurriedly. Thomas does not seem phased by my delayed response.

He smiles warmly. "You too, dear. I look forward to having you in my sessions."

Once out the door of the crafts room, Lacey excitedly jerks on my arm. "I'm so proud of you, June! Tom was the one not sure about having an intern listen in on his time with the doctors, but you have already been granted permission. Your spark of kindness, and thoughtful attitude is just what these patients need. I just know it!" She exclaims. *Hmmm guess I am the true treatment*. These patients just needed a little June in their lives. I cannot help but giggle at my egotistical thoughts as I remember the current month is in fact, June.

Two patients are all for today. Sadly, Lacey is leaving early to eat with her husband. So selfish, spending time with her loved ones. How could she? Okay, I am joshing but still, this means I am on my own for dinner. Juvenile as it may sound, I am terrified of walking into that cafeteria, and dining alone. I feel like I am back at school as I rub my clammy palms on the back of my itchy scrubs.

I look over the cafeteria lines, trying to decide on a meal, when I notice the cute intern, Evan, receiving a scoop of powdery mashed potatoes. My nervous feelings multiply. I am tempted to walk back out, and feast on granola in my room. *No no no*. I am going to be a grown up now. I am going to claw my way out of my water-well resembling comfort zone.

I quickly stride over and grab a tray at the salad bar, in order to intercept Evan as he exits the homestyle line. To my delight, he actually acknowledges me first.

"Hey, Juney-B! How's it going?" *Oh no. I do not have a script prepared for this encounter. Lord, please give me some dialogue.*

"Oh, you know it's going!" *What?* I have never used that cheeky phrase in my whole life. "Things are definitely things." *And we are back to the social awkwardness.* "Uh, it's Ella by the way. So, I'm Juney-E!" I tell him as I sprinkle a pound of parmesan cheese onto the caesar salad I am currently creating.

"Ella, I like it! So, if it's June E then you really are Juney?" He jokes as we swipe our cards and head for a table.

"That I am! It's funny my mi– oldest. My oldest sister is named Elizabeth. My mom wanted her to be called Ella for short, but then everybody just assumed it was Lizzie. So that was more her name. My mom really loved Ella, though, so I kind of got a hand me down middle name." *I guess I am going to pretend Addison is Elizabeth now?*

Evan chuckles before asking the most forward question ever to request an answer from me. "That's great. Is your sister as pretty as you?" *Well she's dead, so at this point, probably not.*

"Uh much prettier, actually. Shiny blonde hair, tan, light blue eyes. She's gorgeous." I admit, pretending for a moment that it was still true.

"But June, how can you even compare blonde to your breathtaking red?" Evan asks, not faltering on the flattery. It is a little bit of an intense approach, but I'm a fan.

"Yeah right," I respond. "More like the red-headed stepchild."

Evan's smile furthers. "C'mon June, you're a middle child. That is far worse than a stepchild."

My fork and I play toss with a wrinkly cherry tomato before I reply. "Well, sometimes I wonder if my parents ever really liked me. My last name is Wilson. Soooo, Ella may sound elegant, but it makes my initials, Jew."

Evan snorts on his soda, his bubbly laughter contagious. "So, your parents aren't a fan of eugenics?!" From the moment that question slips from his soft-looking lips, I know Evan may be my kind of crazy.

Evan offers to walk me back to my room. Well, his room is diagonal to mine, so not really much of a sacrifice but still, it is sweet. When we get to the door, he gives me this look. One impossible to describe. Cheesy as it sounds, the look makes me feel... pretty. Evan hugs me, before moseying over to his side of the hall. For the first time, in a long time, I climb into bed feeling good about myself.

# CHAPTER SIX: UNSETTLED

I may have drifted to sleep feeling light as air, but I awake the following morning with a heart as heavy as stone. Meeting Thomas frenzied my mind with unpleasant thoughts. The truly antagonizing one being whether or not I would rather my sister be dead or impaired. Not impaired like Thomas, if that was the case, I would without a doubt want Elizabeth here. The kind of disability I am pondering is detrimental.

I am unable to get this one story about a girl I went to elementary school with out of my head. Her mother was nearly killed in an accident. When I say nearly killed, I mean they were getting funeral arrangements prepared by the time they found out she had a slight chance of survival. Her mother surfaced from the incident as an entirely altered person. She is thoroughly paralyzed from the neck down and can barely muster audible sounds, let alone words. Her thoughts are not complete. Her memory practically lost. The majority of the time, she is in a state of incoherence. Regardless of her condition, she still maintains a presence. From a wheelchair, she has been at all of her children's birthdays, sporting events, and even witnessed her daughter graduate. She may even attend her kids' weddings and meet her grandchildren.

The same girl's father passed away when I was in middle school. He threw himself off an office building in Atlanta, the city they had moved to in order to secure better medical care for her mother. It was devastating for that family. I cannot help but wonder though, which outcome of the girl's parents is preferable.

Would it have been better that Lizzie's accident cause severe damage due to lack of oxygen to the brain? Would I rather her be barely alive or dead? I know I will never know the answer, nobody can. There is no way that girl knows what she would rather have happened, even though she is living with both scenarios.

*Fun morning thoughts.* Though it is thirty minutes before my alarm is set to go off, I decide, for the sake of my sanity, I need to go ahead and hop out of bed. I take an extra-long shower that morning, hoping my pomegranate body wash can cleanse not only my body but my mind.

Lacey misses breakfast, which I actually do not mind. Evan and I eat together again. He tells me all about his meeting with Pearl. Apparently, she really does have a taste for young bachelors. He says that she was fawning all over him, even pinching his biceps at one point. He was utterly creeped out but said he planned to use it to his advantage. Get more into her psyche. I secretly think he enjoys the extra attention a bit. I cannot blame Pearl though; the boy is a looker.

Lacey shows up at the end of the meal, seeming very happy with me and Evan sitting together. "Look at you babies, bonding! Hate to break up the party but, June, Mr. Creed will probably be expecting us soon."

"Oh, you're meeting Randall today? Super chill guy!" Adds Evan.

I really am looking forward to seeing Randall again. He seems interesting, even wise. I tell Evan goodbye. We agree to eat dinner together again tonight.

"Randall has coffee most mornings in the sunroom. He likes to look out over the woods. There is a nice view, you can even see part of the creek out back, through the sunroom windows. It calms him." Lacey tells me as we walk.

"Good morning ladies. How are you today?" Randall inquires, his eyes lighting up eagerly when he sees us.

"We are fantastic, Randall! You remember Miss June from yesterday?" Lacey asks.

"The intelligent intern, of course." He responds, his smile radiating warmth at me.

"Hi, Mr. Creed. So nice to see you again." I say, feeling oddly at ease.

"So, Randall, I thought maybe you could give June a little background about yourself. Then a few insights, so she is not too lost during our sessions. Also, if you would like to give her any preferences you are welcome to." Lacey tells him, diving right in. She gave this speech to the other two patients I met. I assume it to be standard procedure, but the formality of it still puts me a little on edge. Perhaps, that is the point. I am not supposed to be overly comfortable.

"Lacey don't make me out to be too fascinating now," Randall responds with a laugh. "June, I'm insane. I know how that sounds, but it is the truth. I am certifiably psychotic. Please, don't be scared of me. I'm not a maniac. Just keep in mind, if I say something that does not make sense, it's not on purpose. If I start to panic, it is not your fault and never will be. It's important you know that." I am impressed with how forward he is being, without making me feel anomalous. What he says makes complete sense. In fact, it is actually incredibly considerate, seeing that I am supposed to be the one learning how to make him feel better.

"So, my background," Randall starts. "I am from Tuscaloosa; my parents live a half hour away. I love my parents dearly. I have a big brother who lives in Georgia, and a little sister, who you remind me a lot of, that is a sophomore in high school. I graduated almost five years ago from UA. *Roll tide*." I chuckle as he does a mock country accent. "I got a Literature degree. I know what you're thinking, 'how are you going to make a living with that degree?' Well, I did not. I wanted to be a journalist. I really wanted to write about the truth, June. Turns out, the only real truth is that normalcy is a lie." This statement pricks my neck with chills as it is far from false.

"I've always had some issues. I do not process

things the way people ordinarily do. The sadness and fear people feel in certain situations are exemplified in my mind. Some days, I feel as if those feelings are swallowing me whole. Growing up, I could manage them, even until a couple of years ago I could.

"I made a choice to go into the military after I graduate. I wanted structure, maybe even wanted something to write about." As Randall says this his voice lowers. He begins to look out the window distractedly. I feel an instant closeness to him knowing he has had military involvement because I am reminded of my brother Jamie, who also joined for reasons difficult to explain. After a moment, Randall seems to hear an internal snap. He blinks hard before resuming his speech.

"That was in 2002 when everything was so messy. I went overseas, and well, to sum it up, something very, very awful happened. I returned to the US with severe symptoms of PTSD. That is how I wound up here. You see those emotions I mentioned? They infected me. After the incident, I could not cleanse my system of the sorrow, and dread, and guilt. Those feelings have been permanently branded into my soul. Sadly, they do not make an antibiotic for sickly emotions. I feel like my body will never be relieved of these feelings, which is terrifying." I can see Randall's eyes dampening as he speaks, his voice shaky.

Lacey can tell he is getting triggered. She knows it is time to intervene. "Randall tries so hard every day to feel better, though. He is the strongest person I have ever met." Lacey amends as she lightly rubs his arm. Randall looks at her, a shadow of a smile cast upon his face.

"Thank you, Lacey. Sorry, June. I just get a bit off track sometimes. My mind gets ahead of me," admits Randall.

Little do I know how accurate his statement is. I will come to find out that Randall suffers from rapidly overlapping thoughts, that are sometimes contagious. He is brilliant and thinks of things average people never consider. It breaks my heart that they are the same thoughts almost impossible to get past.

"Some advice I will recommend is to be patient. Not just with me, but with all the folks here. It can be tedious to hear somebody else's thinking patterns, but I promise it can be very intriguing. Which I'm sure you know June, you want to be a psychologist, right?" Randall inquires.

For the next hour, he simply asks me questions about myself. He tells me about his sister. We share some stories centered around the struggles of growing up in the rural south, like getting stuck behind a tractor on the way to school. Talking with Randall is effortless, conversation flows like a river. Lacey drifts into a light lull as we speak. She scares us both by jumping up suddenly as her beeper goes off.

"Oh, my goodness, time has just run from us, now hasn't it?! Randall, we have to go hun, but, if you are okay with it, I am going to drop June off for your session with Dr. Brooks at 2?" Lacey exclaims, tripping over her words like tumbling dominoes as she realizes her schedule is now rushed.

"I would love that." Randall agrees. This makes me feel so valid as a person. That may sound strange, but I feel worthy since an individual I have just met feels so comfortable with me. I tell Randall goodbye, genuinely ecstatic to be listening in on my first session of the summer in just a few hours.

Unfortunately, that is not my first session. I actually end up sitting in right after meeting with Randall. Lacey and I were supposed to meet Glinda 30 minutes earlier, but because we lost track of time, that did not happen. Lacey's plan was for me to meet her, and then see if she would let me sit in on her morning session immediately after. We approach Glinda about five minutes before her therapy session. Though she has not met me, which obviously makes her unhappy, she still allows me to observe. It is the most draining ninety minutes fathomable.

Lacey warned me as we were speed-walking to meet Glinda that she suffers from multiple personality disorder. About forty-five minutes into her therapy session, I realize it is a hoax. I am not being overly-critical, a decent percentage of people diagnosed with multiple personality disorder have admitted to faking. It is not true in all cases; a lot of people truly suffer from this disease. Glinda is very obviously putting on a charade, though.

She has three personalities. Glinda, Macey, and Leslie. Sadly, none of her personalities are the "good witch." She is only a cold bitch. I am blown away when she admits to falsifying her disease, mid-therapy session. Little do I know, it will morph into a reoccurrence.

Apparently, if Glinda is simply Glinda, and nobody else, she will be an average person. She confesses to not wanting to face normalcy. How is this okay? *She says she is faking; shouldn't she go home now?*

In the following days, I start to notice the depth of her ludicrousy. She always admits during therapy, but never, ever, breaks the facade outside of that room. Though the doctors know what she is up to, the other patients are firmly kept in the dark. She seems to adore having them fooled, craves the attention. I realize anytime she is in the craft room or outside, she will have a little clique flanking her. *An entourage of mentally-insane-homies.* If they stop paying her mind, then she will immediately flip personalities like an automated light switch. It is baffling that the patients do not notice it.

I have a conversation with Lacey after witnessing four of Glinda's sessions. Her insight being, "well dear, that's why she is here. Anybody who tries that desperately to fool others is not well in the head. You must think of her as a sociopath rather than a sufferer of DID. If you ask me, compulsive lying is one of the most detrimental disorders."

What Lacey says makes complete sense, however, it does not mean I have to respect Glinda the way I respect other patients like Randall.

# CHAPTER 7: MOONSTRUCK

When Lacey tells me this of Glinda, it is almost close to supper time. Lacey informs me she is going home for dinner. Over the past week, she has done this about four times, which is fine with me. It usually means Evan and I get some alone time. That is, if we are on the same dinner shift. Unfortunately, he had told me the night before that he was sitting in on a late session with Tom and was having to go to dinner at a later time than usual. We are assigned shifts to keep the system running smoothly. Tonight, I have 7:30 and Evan has 8:30.

As I start in the direction of the cafeteria, I realize my stomach is not even yearning for food. I am exhausted. These early mornings are draining energy from my body like a vampire sucking blood. I am also still full from the meatloaf sandwich I scarfed down for lunch. Instead, I decide to retreat to my room like a little wounded puppy.

Upon arrival, I peel off my scrubs, rinse off quickly, not washing my hair, and jump right into bed. I switch on a sitcom, snuggle in under my blankets, and knock out like a hibernating grizzly bear.

My soul leaps from my body in fear when a robust knock makes a thud against my door. That sounds like an exaggeration, but I am telling you, my entire being is startled. My cobalt-blue eyes, jam-packed with stinging sleep, scan the room cautiously. Not aware of what is happening. As I hear the knock a second time, my ears also pick up a voice. "Juneyyyyy." I hear being cooed through the solid wood.

A tidal wave of alertness washes through my brain. *Evan is at my door. Evan might have a skeleton key, and can actually open said door before I can. The only thing on my body is a pair of tiger-striped panties.*

"Hold on! I'm coming." I yell, searching frantically for an article of clothing. Worried because my family always tells me my version of being loud is practically inaudible. I grab a faded hoodie that has an American flag on it, and throw on a pair of jogging shorts before stumbling to the door and swinging it open.

There stands Evan, tall and delicious. His kind-looking eyes light up once he sees me, and babbling immediately escapes from his mouth, "June, I'm calling on you for a reason. You see, if I eat one more bite of bland food from the cafeteria, I will surely perish. I have a feeling the ladies even use a pinch of arsenic to spice up the broccoli casserole. I know you have already eaten, but would you care to join me on the quest for edible food items?"

*Arsenic. My heart.*

"Well Evan, I actually have not eaten. I chose sleep over stale dinner-rolls. Come to think of it, I'm downright famished. I would be delighted to join you on this adventure. Just, uh let me put on actual clothes, please." I say, trying to conceal just how excited I truly am.

"Alrighty," replies Evan with a crooked smile. He pushes past me and into my room. The boy is not shy. Guess I am getting dressed in the closet.

Evan begins making the two stuffed animals on my bed, Tigee and Leppy (bet you can't figure out what animals they are), talk to one another.

As I pull on a pair of ripped jeans and a violet camisole, I hear, "oh hello, leopard would you care for some tea?" Then in a different tone, "oh yes Tiger that would be wonderful, do you have any crumpets?" I instantly crack up.

"I hate to break up the party, but I think we need food, sir," I say as I grab my purse.

"Yes ma'am," agrees Evan, gently setting down the plush critters. As I approach the door, Evan runs around my side and intercepts me, blocking the exit.

"What's up?" I ask, completely caught off guard.

"June, what are you thinking?! If we are ever going to escape this place, we have to be cautious. They are watching us." *Oh Lord, guess we are patients now.*

"Okay," I whisper back. "You lead the way."

Down the hall, we sneak, our backs flat against the wall. Evan covers his lips with one finger before looking around the corner that leads to the stairs. He silently ushers me to follow, and we tiptoe to the stairwell. At the bottom, he places his hands firmly on either side of my shoulders. Evan looks at me, dead serious. "Now these are the offices. This is the hard part. Our whole plan comes down to this moment. To avoid noise, we must take off our shoes and slide on our socks through the foyer. It's the only way, June."

Evan does not so much as falter his poker face with a hint of a smile. I, on the other hand, can taste salty blood from where I have bitten the inside of my mouth to keep from busting out in loud, hysterical laughter. I do what is asked of me and take off my shoes. I fear he may judge me for my completely mismatched socks, but he is so focused on the game I could have taken off my shirt, and he would not have batted an eye.

We skate across the slick floor, me praying that I will not fall and humiliate myself. Finally, we make it to the exit of Maze. We slip our shoes back on and bolt to Evan's rental truck. He spins out of the parking lot, dramatically slinging gravel. He rolls down the window and hollers, "you'll never catch us alive!!" *This is going to be a great night.*

"So Juney-E, where do ya wanna eat?" Evan asks. Apparently, he is unaware that for a girl, picking a restaurant is more difficult than honors calculus.

"Uhhhh, anything is fine with me. You choose!" I say, staying true to the stereotype.

As we approach town, I can see fast food is most likely the only option. "Hmmm, we have burger places, pizza, Waffle Mansion. What in the world is Waffle Mansion?" Evan inquires, raising an eyebrow.

"Are you kidding me? You have never had Waffle Mansion?!" I exclaim in mock horror. I know he is not from the South, but still never having the greasy wonder that is Waffle Mansion food? That hurts my heart.

"Well, I'm going to have it now." Evan decides as he swerves into the restaurant's parking lot.

I know I should probably warn him before we proceed. "Keep in mind though, it's best after midnight when you are drunk. It's kind of like sending your kid to preschool to be around germs. It may not be the cleanest, but it will build up your immune system."

Evan's eyes widen to reveal more white, as he responds. "Girl, you trying to kill me?"

We sit down and glance over the menu before a toothless waitress hobbles over to take our order. Evan asks for standard hash browns. I have to intervene, and tell her he wants them, "scattered well."

"You are cute when you order for me," says Evan with a wink.

"I try," I respond timidly. "So, who made you want to come to Maze?"

"My uncle, remember?" Evan inquires, a little confused.

"Yeah, but who really made you fascinated with the human mind? We all have our technical reasons, but people don't just seek out an internship at a mental institution. We all have our favorite lunatic, who is yours? Who made you want to be a sociologist?"

"Hmmmmm. Is Hitler too mainstream?"

"I mean you are talking to a Jew, remember?"

"Oh, good point! Well, I guess I'm going to go with Charlie Chaplin then." He says, seriously.

I almost spit out my sweet tea. "What in the world are you talking about?"

Evan raises his eyebrows. "You didn't know Chaplin was a psycho?"

"Elaborate." I urge.

"When women would audition for roles in his movies, he would demand they strip naked, sit on a couch, and let him pelt them with cream pies to test their 'chemistry.'" Evan makes air quotations over the final word.

"Wow, thanks for ruining my childhood, Evan," I mumble.

"I got you, girl." He chuckles.

Our waitress sets down our steaming, questionably nutritious, but totally delicious food. I squirt ketchup onto my crispy hash browns, the initial clear juice, infected with red specks, splashing against my shirt. *Quite the graceful creature.*

"Okay Miss Smarts, who made you fall in love with insanity? A serial killer?" Evan asks as he flicks a straw wrapper at me.

"Ohhhhh, I'm a Rasputin girl, for sure. Hands down. Love me some Grigori." I inform him.

Evan's composure slips. He covers his red face with a napkin as he tries to control his choking laughter.

"What?" I ask, slightly self-conscious, but also snickering. "He is a crazy wizard who walked from Siberia to Moscow in the dead of winter! God knows, what it was like in his mind."

Evan finally looks up at me, I can see tears of amusement rolling down his tan cheeks. "No, Juney. I don't judge your choice. It's just… I never thought a girl would bring-up the Russian Revolution on a first date. I mean where have you been all my life?" He sends a happy wink my way. "Wanna talk about Stalin?"

"Oh boy, did you just open up a can of worms." We spend the next two hours rambling about oddities and laughing until my stomach ached. I had not originally realized it was a date, but it turned out to be the best one I could ever hope to have.

That night, when Evan walks me to my room, he stops in between our doors. His hands softly hold mine. His thumb reassuringly caressing my own. I can feel his body heat radiating as he leans into me. I lift my head and finally make acquaintance with his silky-smooth lips.

That is my first kiss with Evan, but more remarkably, it is my first kiss in an insane asylum.

# CHAPTER EIGHT: TOUCHED

As the weeks fly by, I realize outdoor time is definitely the best way to connect with patients. It is the least regulated of our activities. I loathe the field trips. Imagine visiting a messy store with seven people that have OCD. *Not fun.* I also have to admit, I do not adore the craft room. Patients get... bizarre in there. The drawings are not always appropriate if you catch my drift. Especially not for an 18-year-old virgin. *Or anyone not into bestiality.*

The only time I enjoy crafting is when Randall is in there painting. It is soothing to watch him fabricate scenes that are breathtaking in their simplicity. Randall loves nature. He often paints brooks and streams, sometimes autumn trees losing leaves. He has an air of tranquility that makes even anxious me feel a flush of peace.

I create a habit of walking Randall back to his room after his sessions. I start referring to this as Dr. Randall's sessions with me because when I would talk, he would listen intently. I seldom have to wait for him to regain interest or spice up the subject to keep his attention hooked. Randall morphed into a wonderful confidant.

It was two weeks into the program when Randall and I had a conversation proving how much we have in common in terms of parallel thinking patterns. To be blunt, he just cannot get a grip on his. We talked about the need for depth in this world. I confessed to him that I think, possibly, the "deepness" I am referring to is actually depression disorder.

We agreed it is only considered that by a social standard. The general population can be simple-minded enough to cast off people who read between the lines or ask a few too many questions as perpetually depressed. I hope that some of those people are like me and just handle, struggle, but handle that diversion from society. Yet, I have a theory that eventually these people cannot handle being so different and lose themselves entirely.

Randall told me he felt like they "float too far from reason." Then they end up being deemed insane, lunatics even, and sent somewhere like Maze. Randall thinks he is a prime example of this.

I would hate to make him feel outcasted in any way because he should not be. I told him my honest opinion, that maybe society needs to depress themselves a little bit in order to improve civilization as a whole. That depth should no longer be written off as a mental illness but be the new normal. It may be harsh but it's realistic, and it is fair. Then, we can focus on correcting some of the fault in our world instead of simply turning a blind eye to it. Disorders do exist, and they do matter. Randall added that if we never fix the underlying problems, then the world may end up at war yet again.

When he said this, I was reminded of his experience with the military. Shoot me for being nosy, but curiosity is consuming me about what exactly had happened to rattle Randall to such a degree. That day was not the right one to ask. This conversation as a whole makes me feel like I am not the only one. What more can I ask for?

One patient was not taking to me quite as well. Thomas's manic episodes had worsened, especially towards women. I only ended up sitting in on a handful of his sessions. On my fifth, I could immediately tell it was not going to be a good one. My eyes gravitated like active magnets to the faint red circles adorning his temples. Evidence of shock therapy.

Not so fun family fact: I recognized them so quickly because my grandfather underwent shock therapy right before his death. It was 1990; I was three. He had been frolicking in his neighbor's garden around 4 AM, one winter night. Would not have been quite as big of a deal if he had not been naked, except for earmuffs. He would not listen to anybody. Eventually, even though they did not want, the neighbors called the police. The sad part is, he just had dementia.

My grandmother, however, was lost in a sea of indefinite denial.

She wanted him to have had a psychotic breakdown so that there could be treatment. She was unable to cope with the fact that his mind was wasting away. Since she was deemed his caregiver, she pushed for shock therapy, and the doctors abided. It was honestly just heartbreaking for all involved. My parents took me to see him pretty soon after that. Guess they realized things were going downhill. One of my first memories is a wrinkled man with jaundiced skin and an electric shock halo. He died of a stroke two months later. My grandmother is now on one of those elderly cruises. *The ones where they keep an incinerator aboard.*

So, I instantly knew what Tom had been subjected to. My lungs felt heavy with genuine empathy. These days, institutions do not use that form of treatment unless the patient has taken a severe turn. My empathy was joined by discomfort as I noticed Tom's eyes kept gravitating toward me during the session. That and the fact that his tongue would not stay in his drooling mouth. Every question Dr. Brooks asked, Tom, proceeded with, "if June doesn't mind." *Excuse me?*

At the end of the session, as I was trying to flee the scene, I noticed Thomas whisper something into Dr. Brooks' ear. Something that made the doctor's eyes bulge from their sockets. An orderly walked Tom backed to his room. Lacey was paged to Dr. Brooks' room. I waited in the hall while they engaged in an intense chat. She emerged with a smile, but I could see the corners of her lips quivering.

"What's going on?" I inquired, apprehensively.

"Oh nothing, dear. It's just well… Thomas kind

of wants to… Keep a lock of your hair." Lacey fidgets with her name tag.

"Oh. Well, that's not that bad." I say with relief.

"After he's cut off your head." *Oh, okay then.*

After a solid minute of silence, she speaks again.

"Yeah, so we are just going to stick with the other three from now on."

"Good idea." I agree, preferring my head and neck to be attached. She gives me a quick embrace before sliding her arm through mine and guiding me towards the cafeteria.

"Patients say the darndest things sometimes! I promise we have only had one employee fatality, and he was a jerk anyhow." She coos. I cringe. "I'm gonna get you an ice cream cone. How about that, dollface?"

That's when I realize that no matter how old I get, frozen dairy treats will continue to fix anything and everything.

# CHAPTER NINE: BATTY

A week later, I have the privilege of dealing with another patient oddity. I sit in on the most absurd session with Glinda. The most pointless session in existence. One that makes me question pursuing psychology.

You see, there is a summer cold going around Maze. Thankfully, the interns have all managed to avoid it, but Glinda is not as lucky.

Glinda apparently has a tendency of getting laryngitis in unison with a cold. As a result, once she has gotten through the preliminary stages of her illness, her vocal cords, dry and damaged, give out causing her to lose her voice. Let's be real, nobody every fully loses it, it just becomes extremely strained. Sensible people desire to rest their swollen vocals. Glinda wants that as well, but for some odd reason, demands to still have therapy. But not only can she barely speak, but she is also purposefully refraining from it in order to heal.

Sooooo, she, Dr. Mosh, and I sit for a fifty-minute session without her uttering a single word. Literally not a one. She just has a piece of paper that she can scribble on. When the Doctor asks if she wants to end the session, she scribbles "NO." Only word written the whole session. *Consider my patience tested.*

Glinda's session has me positively peeved, and not at all looking forward to Pearl's one in a few hours. I like Pearl fine, I am a little scared she is going to shank me, but all in all she is a nice lady. I am pleasantly surprised with her session that day as it becomes centered around her family.

Pearl does not volunteer to tell me her life's story. I instead hear it through a series of questions by Dr. Mosh. He starts out with, "Pearl do you miss Arkansas?"

"No. It was muddy and smelt like sewer. We ain't had nothing growing up. I miss Vegas." She replies, in desperate need of a grammar lesson.

Dr. Mosh, still fixated on Arkansas, continues. "Pearl, you told me once that you and your siblings had to plead for everything. I think a can of wet dog food was your example. How did that make you feel?"

Pearl takes a moment to reflect. Her eyes glaze over like fresh donuts, and she begins scanning the room as if seeking an emergency exit. "It made me want to leave."

"What did you do when you got to Nevada?" Dr. Mosh asks.

"Become a showgirl." Pearl's tone implying she finds his question to be of a dumbass nature.

"Can you define showgirl for me, please?" He

inquires. Literally the most psychologist sounding question I can fathom.

"Doctor, it's somebody that puts on a show. A person who wakes up every morning and makes themselves what others desire. It's caking on slabs of make-up to entertain the wealthy. It is vomiting up meals to keep a slim, and therefore desirable, figure. It is getting infections from overuse of eyelash glue. It is looking out over a sea of people that look at you with amazement as your blistered feet ache and your smile, the smile that sells the whole act, makes your jaw terribly sore. That's what being a showgirl means." Pearl states with more energy than I have ever seen her muster. Her chocolate colored eyes twitch, and her lips quiver as she takes in the gravity of the literal Hell she has just described. That Hell being her life, her legacy.

My heart breaks when she starts to cry softly. She seems to pull a light pink handkerchief covered in daisies out of thin air and holds it to her dripping nose. She then looks up suddenly. "Is my husband here yet?"

A tree branch fell on her husband's car seven months after she was checked into Maze. A limb impaled his abdomen, causing him to bleed out before the paramedics could clear the branches and get to him.

I have no idea how much of this Pearl knows. I assume they told her he moved to Heaven. She asks for him sometimes, but I do not think it is because she cannot process his actual death. I think she wants to push off the realization that he is never coming back for her. Pearl's fate was sealed the moment the pine shattered his windshield. She is staying at Maze. That is much too difficult for her to face.

Her session sinks into me as I walk to the cafeteria for dinner. I pick at a piece of gummy porkchop as I sit, lost in a haze of thoughts. Evan is a little down because I am not being conversational in the slightest. He is trying to tell me about the first time he walked in on his parents getting high.

"So, get this Juney, I run into their bedroom to ask if my mom can warm me up some mac and cheese. I'm only eight remember. It looks like cold air coming-off-ice has filled the room. It smells like a skunk baked into a lemon pie. Not the most pleasant scent.

"Then my mother gets all…. Earthy? She says, I remember it vividly, 'honey you know how veggies nurture your body? Well, certain grasses nurture your mind. But only when you are a grown-up, sometimes our brains need a little help.' Then they took me into the kitchen to warm up my macaroni, and the stoners ate it all!" He looks at me, amusement sweltering in those seaweed-colored eyes. I feel dreadful when his gaze meets my distracted face, and those same eyes fill with disappointment.

"Evan that's crazy! So funny!" I exclaim, trying to salvage the conversation. Don't get me wrong, it is an amusing story. I just cannot shake the thoughts Pearl's session has evoked about Lizzie from my clouded mind.

"Are you okay, Juney-E? You seem a little... Off." It is sweet of him to notice, but there is no way in Hell I plan on sharing.

I project all my energy into sounding convincing. "I'm just tired. I'll probably go to bed once we are done."

His disappointment turns to sadness. "Are we not snuggling up with a movie tonight? It's Freaky Friday, June."

Since our Waffle Mansion date, so only a few weeks, Evan and I have been renting videos from Maze's little collection. We cannot resist watching one at least three times a week. Freaky Friday, which is our horror movie night, has been a staple since our Saturdays are often free or light schedule-wise. I love it because a boy and I are touching in a bed and laughing and kissing, and I'm being a total girl.

It hurts me to reject Evan, in retrospect, I could use some companionship tonight. Yet, I am craving Benadryl and a sleeping mask. I need an escape into unconsciousness. I risk a white lie and tell him my stomach is hurting me. I do reassure him we will watch an extra film this upcoming week.

I can see in his face that Evan is disheartened. He probably had even ventured out to a convenience store and bought gummies for us to chew on while we watch and cuddle. Evan is thoughtful like that. His firm grip on my hand as he walks me to my door lets me know he understands and is not harboring any hard feelings.

As I am about to lean up and kiss Evan goodnight, I realize his head has already swooped in to place a tender kiss on my nose. Just like a parent would give their baby. He then gently takes my head into his sturdy hands and initiates Eskimo kisses. He reels back, and looks at me, his signature crooked smile gracing his face.

"June, I hope you are okay with being my girl because you just are." Before I can even respond to the best thing my ears have ever heard, he gives me a quick peck on the lips and starts walking towards his room.

I open my door and manage to slide into the room before squealing. I honestly deserve an Oscar for accomplishing such a feat. I pull out my mobile to call my sister and fill her in. My eager fingers push the two on my phone until it becomes an E. Before I get to the L, the sinister reality sinks in. That phone is lying in a shoebox in my mom's closet, dead. Just like its owner.

This sweeps me back to my earlier thoughts. I fall into my bed, hot tears streaming down my face as I let these melancholy emotions engulf me.

My parents were not the most involved. I was young when my sister, Addison, got her driver's license. In return for car payments and gas money, my parents had Addison take over the duty of driving Jamie to and from his football practices. She also took me to and from my dance lessons. *Before I "accidentally" knocked a girl, who told me my face made her want to commit a murder-suicide, off the stage. She was a six-year-old bully whose mom let her watch crime shows.* Still, my parents always came, on time, to his games and my recitals. They would hug us after, but then usually leave, make a date out of the event since they already had a sitter for Delilah.

Addison was left to take out Jamie and his friends for celebratory pizza. She would wipe glitter off my post-show face before taking me for ice cream. I love Addison. I am beyond thankful for everything she has done for me, but it does not mean it was right.

Elizabeth received the opposite treatment from my mom and dad. My mother would take her to cheer practice, but she and my father would seldom attend the actual games she cheered at. Jamie's games were usually a confliction because Jamie went to a different school within our county. They had better sports teams, while mine and my sisters had better academics. They could have alternated, but they told Lizzie it was simple: she was on the sidelines, he was on the field. That was that. I know it broke her heart every time she looked into a crowded stadium void of their faces.

Elizabeth was still the closest to my mom. Driving her to practice and watching her for years, really facilitated their bonding. Even with my dad, Lizzie was still the golden child. She never talked back. She always smiled and laughed at my father's dull jokes. In my family though, the golden child did not get an abundance of special treatment. For the most part, my parents were indifferent to us all. *If they did not want five, maybe they should have tried lambskin instead of ditching condoms all together due to my mother's latex allergy.*

This lack of attention drove Elizabeth mad. So, she rebelled. It was transparent that she would go out of her way to break her preconceived idea of rules. To her dismay, my mother and father could not have cared less. There was nothing for her to disobey because few rules had ever been established. Elizabeth was constantly going out to parties and striving to be the center of attention.

According to believable rumors, Lizzie was the friend who would always accept a dare, no matter how daunting. Her so-called 'pals' thought telling me stories about wild nights, ones where my sister would drink half a keg or initiate a drunken mud fight, would bring me laughter, and therefore comfort. That could not be farther from the truth. I resent any accounts of her acting like an imbecile because that is exactly what got her killed. You would think these high-school-peakers would already understand that, and realize how highly inappropriate their story was, to begin with.

How does this relate to Pearl? Why am I bringing it up? Why am I upset about it? It shows nurture can kill nature. If Pearl had not been treated like dirt when she was a child, then maybe she would not have pursued a career in validation. In her own words, she said her days as a showgirl were torture. It all drove her to be erratic. It all goes back to how she was raised.

Earlier, when I was in Dr. Mosh's therapy room hearing the minutes tick on as Pearl spoke, I made an immediate connection between her and Elizabeth. I became infuriated with both her and my parents. Elizabeth was responsible for her own actions, which makes everything worse because I cannot blame her. She is literally rotting. My parents did start her down this slippery slope, though, by ignoring her self-destructive behavior.

They failed to even try and stop their teenager from guzzling down vodka, at a stranger's house, on a school night. How can I blame them either? Their daughter is worm food.

I sob, and these thoughts eat at me. Her death was so preventable. Eventually, sleep abducts me, but I was not greeted with fairies and rainbows. I am cast into insidiousness.

My soul awakes in what seems like a replayed memory from when Elizabeth and I were children. We are sitting, Indian style, on the carpet of the picturesque bedroom we once shared. It is a mirror image of the original room. Pale-pink-colored wallpaper adorned with intricate white elephants is pasted to the walls. Our twin beds are dressed in matching rose-decorated comforters. My favorite china tea set, the one with the painted lilacs, rests atop our wooden armoire.

We are playing with dolls, making them sing and dance. Our giggles overlap in delight. At first, I am a bystander in the dream. I watch from a distance, but soon I am peering through my own five-year-old eyes. I stare in wonder at Elizabeth's bright, youthful appearance. My mother had pulled her soft golden curls halfway back with an enormous indigo-colored bow. Her aquamarine eyes sparkle as she excitedly shifts her gaze between the dolls and me. My eyes are not glued to her because I am in awe to see her again. On the contrary, immersed in this illusion, I have no idea that she can no longer breath. I am looking at her the way I always looked at her when I was a child. I stare at her with admiration. I used to want nothing more than to be as gorgeous and happy as she always seemed.

We play, me trying to keep up with the conversation Elizabeth's doll is having with mine. I try to focus, but I am distracted by the odd changes starting to occur in the room. The inanimate elephants are now twirling. I glance at our massive armoire. It appears to be going round. The room is spinning. Fuzziness blurs my vision as the speed continues its increase.

Elizabeth does not seem to notice. She ignores me as I become distraught and try to alert her. My sister pulls herself up into a standing position. She carefully begins placing one bare foot after another backwards on the hardwood floor. The closer she gets to the wallpaper, the more it seems like she is being dragged. I fumble on my knees in a desperate attempt to grab her. The winding room welcomes her into its walls slowly, allowing me to see every curl, every finger, every toe become enveloped. She does not call out. Her lips sewn shut. The last features I see are her glittering eyes, beginning to melt like burning candle wax. I hear my tea set shatter. Then the room resumes normalcy while becoming foreign.

My torso bolts from my mattress. My body is slickened with chilly sweat. I can feel my heart attempting to leap from its cage. The attempt at stabilizing my rapid inhales is short-lived when the corner of my eye observes a flicker of movement. A terrified shriek shoots from my throat.

Evan sprints over to me and covers my mouth murmuring "shhhhhh," while rubbing my leg. I can see a pack of antacids in one of his hands, a bottle of ginger ale in the other.

"Easyyyy girl." He whispers without being able to resist a smile. *Did he just call me a horse?*

"It's okay, Juney! I'm sorry I scared you. We just have the skeleton keys, and you didn't answer. I thought surely you weren't asleep at 8:45. But… I guess you were. When I opened the door and saw you jump up, I felt like shit. How are you feeling, beautiful?" Evan asks in what seems like a single breath.

He crawls over me to the other side of the bed and wraps his warm arm around me tightly. He must just think that he has woken me up. Little did he know I was having a nightmare, which is a relief because I do not want to talk about that dream, ever.

"Oh," I mutter. I had forgotten I was supposedly sick. "I feel better, just tired."

Evan pauses and gnaws on his lip for a moment. "You sure you're okay, Juney? You are shaking a lot."

Guess I am not good at concealing my trauma.

"Yeah," I assure weakly. "Hey, Evan? Do you think you could stay with me tonight? I just do not sleep well sometimes… Well, all the time."

Evan pulls me up to lay across his heated body. He begins to comb his fingers through my hair. "June, I'll be here every night if you want me to."

I hug him closer, bury my face in the gap between his neck and shoulder. As I breathe in the comforting aroma of spicy cologne, I begin to drift into a peaceful sleep. I have no more terrorizing dreams that night.

# CHAPTER TEN: SENSELESS

The next morning, I am ripped from slumber by a bizarrely early knock sounding upon my door. As I groggily sit up, my mind is induced into a frenzy knowing that Evan, the only person I would expect, is still fast asleep, drenched in drizzling drool, beside me. He wakes up in a tizzy. I gently push him, intending to simply further his alertness. Instead, accidentally shoving him right off the warm bed. At first, I am smitten with guilt, but then I see him curl up and return to dreamland. I hate to say I am relieved, but I truly am. His silhouette is now perfectly concealed behind the mattress. Unless he starts snoring, which last night proved could be a possibility, his presence will go unnoticed.

I throw on one of my brother's old sweatshirts littering the floor, before swinging open the door to expose Lacey's perpetually cheerful face. She looks ecstatic to tell me whatever news has sent her here.

"You have a visitor dear!!" I look at her gleeful expression, feeling utterly confounded. My eyes stare back at her with vacancy.

"...Lacey who in the world would visit me?" I ask softly, dead serious.

"Oh, my goodness! June you are so silly. You know you come from a big family, right?"

Oh God, which family member is it. A twisted game show in which I, the credulous contestant, can either make a deal to hide or lose. I feel sickening dread enter my system as I imagine the possibility of it being my dad and stepmother.

"June, stop looking at me like I'm a patient! It is just your brother, and boy is he a cutie!" Lacey announces followed by a cringe-worthy wink. Her creepiness aside, I actually feel a surge of relief course through my arteries. I had no clue Jamie would actually have the time to visit me.

I adore my brother, but, quite frankly, video games and girls with low self-esteem seem to absorb his time in between leaves. I cannot blame him; he is a real American hero. He may occupy his downtime with as many counter-productive activities as his somewhat-patriotic heart desires. I tell Lacey I'll be downstairs in ten minutes. She meets me with a squeal of delight. *Lacey is such a good life cheerleader.*

"Uh okay, Bye now," I say awkwardly. Lacey continues to stare as I shut the door. I hurriedly rush over to the still floor-bound Evan, pulling on a change of clothes in the process.

"Evan" I repeat as I give his shoulders a substantial rattle. He groans before finally opening his sleep-swollen eyes.

"Yeah...?" He murmurs, his voice gruff from a

brief lack of use.

"My brother is here! I'm gonna go talk to him. You should go get ready and come down when I text you. I would love for you to at least meet him!" I exclaim, kind of loudly to get through to his slightly-comatose state.

This information makes him lift his head with perk. "Okay, will do." Though I can hear tiredness consuming his voice, I know he is looking forward to it.

I am indifferent to my appearance. It is just my brother, not the Queen. Still, I brush out my hair, put on dark jeans, and an orchid-studded blouse instead of dull, and honestly dirty, scrubs. It feels empowering to dress like an ordinary civilian again.

As I waltz along the hall and hop down the stairwell, I ponder requesting that Randall meet Jamie. I immediately decide against it. I know Randall has military involvement, and I know it is part of the reason he is at Maze. It would kill me for anything about Jamie to be triggering to Randall. I still think they would really like each other though.

When I get to the first level of Maze, my eyes wander enthusiastically around the foyer. In the corner, I can see my big brother twiddling his thumbs while perched on a shiny silver bench. I skip over to him and, once he lifts his gaze to take in my image, am greeted with a crushing hug.

"Jamieeeeeeeee." I screech like a sorority girl. "What are you doing here?"

"Well Juniper, I can't leave the states without telling my favorite cynic bye, now can I? Think it's possible for me to steal you away for some breakfast?" I feel my joy levels spike at the idea of getting out of Maze for a few hours.

"Yep! Give me one sec," I reply, already walking towards the main offices.

Michael sees me before I even pop my head through his door. "I have already cleared it with Lacey, Miss June. Have a fun afternoon!" He says with a grin. He shifts his kind, but obscenely nervous, eyes between the mound of papers on his desk and the glow of his computer monitor.

"Thanks, Michael!" I say though I have already bounced back to Jamie. "Let's go!" I call as I pull Jamie's arm in the direction of the front door.

As I munch on a freshly baked lemon poppy seed muffin, Jamie sets down his latte. He indulges in a stiff inhale before addressing the topic I knew he was avoiding. We spent thirteen years under the same roof. I can read his true emotions like an article trying to appeal to the elderly by utilizing large-sized font.

"Addison's worried about you." He says slowly, mulling over each word with caution.

"And why is that?" I inquire, my tone soaked in blatant unamusement.

"June have you contacted her since you've been here?" Jamie asks. I can arouse no more than an eye roll as I shake my head no.

"Well apparently, she has emailed you some funny videos, or messages asking when she can call. She says you have not been responding except for sending an occasional I love you. She's been dying to visit you but doesn't want to be overbearing. Addison is concerned well, first that you are dead, being ingested by wild dogs. Or more likely, that you are either unhappy here, or so happy that you are wanting to push the family away. After hearing from you how everything's going, sounds like she's right on the latter part." Jamie polishes his statement with a condescending eyebrow raise.

Ugh, am I really going to have to defend myself? I am trying to be independent. His words give me an injection of unsolicited sass.

"Well can she blame me? I am trying to enjoy myself here. Addison is too much. If I talk to her, she's just going to baby me and bring me down. She's so freaking dramatic, Jamie." I plead for him to trim me some slack off of his patronizing steak.

"June, c'mon. Addison loves you. We all do. She is the one who has always been there for you. She pretty much raised you Juniper, you know that. After Lizzie died, she's wanted to take care of you even more." Jamie prods. I am no longer making eye contact with him. My arms are crossed, and my gaze is glued to the dirty coffee-shop floor.

"Now, I know her fussing is obnoxious sometimes. You are just so dear to her June. She wants to make sure you are okay." Jamie continues, a passion highlighting his words. *Is it really necessary to bring Elizabeth into this?* I resent that guilting element of my family. There are four of us still here. Can we forget about the dead one for two fucking seconds?

"I'll talk to her, okay?" I relent in obvious exasperation. "I'm just done with her relating everything about me to Elizabeth. I cannot stand being compared to her any longer, Jamie. I am here doing something totally new and different. Something for myself." I argue, still holding on to a shard of self-defense.

"June, you gotta get over some of the Lizzie stuff. That's just how it is now. You can't hate Addison or mom for finding similarities in y'all. It brings them comfort." He snaps back, not going to give in.

"I am over Elizabeth. I am not going to let her stupidity ruin my entire life. It's bad enough they bawl their freaking eyes out whenever I say a sentence that sounds like 'something Lizzie would say.'" I hold up mock parentheses with my nail-bitten fingers before continuing. "Do you know how many words are in the English language, Jamie? Too many. I can't help but overlap some."

"June, chill-out," Jamie warns.

"No. It's ridiculous. We are totally different people. I look nothing like Lizzie. I am not friendly like her. I do not sing like her or make everybody happy the way she did. I will never be her, and I am secure in that because I will not be dumb like her. I will not be silly or vain like she was. Most importantly I will not make bad choices that get me kil—"

"June!" Jamie interrupts me by violently slamming his fist on the already-wobbly-table. His coffee cup quivers. Strangers are alerted by his ruckus. I lower in my chair.

"This conversation is over. I know you love Elizabeth. I know it is hard to be used as a parallel. However, we are not, you are not, going to bad mouth our sister again. She will never feel, or speak, or be able to defend herself. So what mom mentally puts y'all side by side sometimes? You still have a future. Lizzie does not." Jamie's glare burns into my soul as he speaks, definitely leaving a scar.

We sit in silence for a solid five minutes. "Fallen for any crazies?" He eventually asks.

I chuckle softly. "Not yet."

On the way back to Maze, we continue to focus on light topics. I tell him about Glinda's ludicrous session. He tells me about his ex-girlfriend's pathetic attempt to get back with him. "She sent me a text saying, 'requesting sergeant Jamie Wilson' for plunging duty.' Is that supposed to be sexy? Anyway, I heard she's been sleeping with Mr. Rosin. Remember, he's our neighbor that was required by law to come and tell us he's a pedophile?"

I decide not to mention Evan. I keep from confessing our relationship to Jamie for the sake of everyone's sanity. Keeping my family completely out of the loop is sadly the best option. I feel safer dating Evan knowing he is in the dark, concerning where it is I come from. Introducing him to Jamie could lead to me telling him about Elizabeth or worse; Jamie casually mentioning it as if it is not a foreign subject to Evan. I mean, in Jamie's mind, why should it be? I loved her. *Must mean I want to chat about her with eligible bachelors.*

When you conceal a little of the truth to somebody, you cannot let your guard down without risking imminent exposure.

"Well thank you so much for coming to see

me," I tell Jamie as he returns me to my asylum. "It really means a lot."

"Of course, Juniper. I really am glad you are here, trying something different. God knows that high school did not treat you well. I saw one of those girls the other day." My ears perk, and my cheeks flush. "Would have told her to go screw herself, but she was at the store with her grandmother or some ancient woman. Looked like she could have gone to school with Lincoln. Anyway, didn't want to give the hag a heart-attack so I refrained. If it is any consolation, the girl is a total heifer now." Jamie is referring to Denise. A girl who tormented me after Elizabeth's death. She graduated two years ago. Her expedited weight gain does bring me a twisted sense of pleasure.

"Hmmm sounds like her granny was at the wrong place at the wrong time. Thank you though, Jamie. And I'm sorry about earlier, I just…" My words dwindle.

"It's okay, June. I know you." He pulls me in for a tight squeeze and places a peck on my matted hair.

"Be really safe over there, Jamie. Give those terrorists something to terrorize about." *Yeah, I know nothing about the current military situation. I just know three years ago, shit hit the fan.* "I love you, bro."

"I love you too, psycho." He says with a chuckle. "See ya, back home. At… some point." I see an ounce of disturbia settle into his grey eyes. Jamie has no idea when he will return. We both know, as much as it makes me feel like I am suffocating, that he might not.

I step out onto Maze's front steps to watch him drive away. He drifts back to his brutal reality. Jamie's world is so much harsher than mine. Yet, I am so much more pessimistic than him. *Sometimes I hate June Wilson.*

I hobble upstairs, Evan's bedroom being my destination. I knock on his door. "Come in!" I hear in his easy-going voice.

Evan is perched on his bed, typing on a slim laptop. *Dang, I am dating a rich guy*. He is dressed in what I assume to be the nicest clothes he brought to Maze. He looks at me eagerly.

"Can I meet him now?" Evan asks. I immediately feel my heart wrench, like somebody is digging their sharp fingernails into the soft tissue. I run over to hug him, almost in tears.

"Whoa whoa. What's wrong Juney?" He queries, totally bewildered.

"Nothing. He just got a text and had to leave super soon, or his transportation would be messed up. I'm so sorry, Evan." I cry, trying to fabricate an excuse.

"Awh June don't worry about me. It's no big deal. I am sure you are sad he's deploying again." His soothing tone is surreal in its warmth.

"It's so hard." I offer. In a way, except for that fleeting moment of soul-crushing fear I experienced when he left, I am numb to Jamie leaving the country. I am sniveling because I am so sad to have two people I care about in the same building and not be able to let them meet. *I still blame Elizabeth.*

# CHAPTER ELEVEN: BESIDE ONESELF

Jamie's visit muddles my ability to filter. The next day, when I am strolling Maze's yard with Randall, I start to slur the blurred lines of appropriate speech. Earlier that afternoon, I had been in Randall's session with Dr. Mosh. A hint was dropped as an afterthought, like water dripping from an-almost-turned-off-faucet, concerning Randall's past. As we walk the little loop of a trail that diverts through the woods, giving patients a slight illusion of freedom, I cross my preconceived boundary. Perhaps growing accustomed to an environment in which people are constantly encouraged to speak their minds is not the best idea for me. I just feel like I can comprehend Randall better if I understand. Obviously, the doctors prod. I am his ally, why can't I?

"Randall, Dr. Mosh said you have to get over your fear of authority. That it sprouted in the military and should be overturned. What was he implying?" I inquire bravely.

He is even more brave in responding. "Well June, I made a rash decision about three and a half years ago. After a few months of being a lack-luster journalist with no solid job opportunities, I realized I was truly clueless as to where I was going with my life. I had a girlfriend at the time. One day, she met me at a little coffee shop near my apartment. We sipped on cappuccinos by the restaurant's cozy fireplace as she came to what she thought was a grand solution. That I should join the military, more specifically the army." I raise an eyebrow at him. Confounded as to how she came to such a bold conclusion.

"Oh, June." He seems to realize I may need a time warning. "I'll tell you all this, but it is going to take a minute. Trust me." I nod.

"So, I know what you're thinking. In her mind, though, she assumed a routine lifestyle would help ground me. 'Keep me bound to society', she said. 9/11 had just happened. America seemed to be falling apart. At the time I was athletic. I was very involved in my college's swim team. Even won all-state my junior year. To me, her thinking me worthy of the military was such an honor. I felt like she really believed in me, and perhaps she did." He kind of hesitates, digging his worn sneakers into the earthy ground. "...she just didn't believe that I could get better after I was discharged less than three years later. I gave it my all June. I excelled at basic. I was looked at as prestigious and motivated, so I gained more privileges quickly. Except in my eyes, they were not exactly privileges. I did not desire leadership duties. I did not expect to be sent overseas so quickly. I did not want to be looked at as such a heroic man. Honestly, I was trying to fit in. I did what I was told because I thought it would simply make me another cadet." Instead of just pausing, he decides to sit criss-cross on the shaded path. That way, we could continue our conversation in private and avoid returning to the others.

"I had a friend who was very dear to me, his name was Simon. We were bunkmates after being deployed to Afghanistan. We became like brothers…. Long days. The military is full of those. And little sleep. One night, Simon, a few of our other team members, and I were crashing at an abandoned building. This was over a year and a half in, we had recently been transferred to Iraq.

"The place was super tiny and cramped, but it was safe. The building had been cleared, and we were desperate for an ounce of shut-eye. We decided to alternate lookout. A lookout is always necessary. Enemies can pop out of nowhere. It's just this time, we seemed to be so alone. In a ghost town. I was first lookout. We settled in at about one in the morning, and I agreed to stay up until four. Around two, my consciousness started to dwindle.

"I began drifting in and out of a light lull, helplessly. Honestly June, I really was not throwing caution to the wind. It was innocent. A total accident, I swear." His broken expression pleads with me to believe him. *Of course, I did.*

"Randall, I know. I would never judge you", I assure. I place my steady hand over his trembling one.

He takes these words as encouragement and continues. "It was probably thirty minutes later when I awoke fully to shots and screaming. We had been followed. I had been sent to keep watch from the front window, while everybody else slept in the room over. The shooters had attacked from the back. I ran towards the deafening noise. Gunfire studded the walls, consuming them like moths feeding on sweaters.

"I dropped to the floor and was met by three bodies. The ensuing powder was thick, but I could see that Simon had just hit the ground. I crawled towards him. A burning sensation surged through my ear, but I ignored it. Simon's petrified eyes displayed cold suffocation before becoming glassy and opaque. Blood flooded from his torn chest. The other boys laid motionless. I saw a gun in each of their hands. They had gotten to their feet, or begun to, before I even woke up."

I can see Randall's heart racing through his aquamarine eyes as he speaks. "Just then, I heard footsteps approaching. I instinctively laid my head back down. Shut my eyes tightly. Slowed my breathing. Played opossum."

"I heard foreign language spewing, and interest evaporating as the men kicked at us. They thought me to be dead, and I thought them to be leaving. Suddenly, another shot sounded right beside my stinging ear. Simon's stringy brains embedded with crumbled skull coated my face. Not flinching in response should have been impossible, but the fear was paralyzing. I waited for them to explode my head for good measure as well. But they were done; I heard them shuffle out not knowing, or not caring, that they had just ripped a father from the world. I think Simon had twitched. Or they did it for sport. But that I can't entertain; I can't believe there could be such evil in this world. I laid there, on that damn dusty floor, consumed in grief for what seemed like days. I couldn't leave them. I had already abandoned them by sleeping. My lack of watch was the reason they were all dead." He takes a moment to steady his trembling lips. His voice cracks with pent-up sorrow as he resumes speaking.

"But eventually, I had to. I had just lost my best friend, along with two other men depending on me. They had all choked-on bullets, their insides ripped and shredded, because my eyes could not stay open."

I gulp hard, but my throat is so void of moisture I feel I will begin coughing up sand.

"I made it back to base in emotional ruins. A piece of my ear had also been blown off during the assault." He pushes back his somewhat-shaggy red hair to reveal a lack of cartilage.

"They hospitalized me. A few days later, I was told I could go home now. I was relieved, but distraught. As I'm sure you can imagine. I have always struggled with mental setbacks. Dealing with this awful, horrid tragedy I had let happen…. That mangled my sanity beyond reverse. I wanted to see my mom but instead was met with interrogations on my return to the state.

"After a few days of cerebral torment, my PTSD was deemed by the government's psychological unit to be too severe to return to society. I was sent to the closest mental institution to my hometown until further improvement. I was sent here, June, months ago. I have had so many failed attempts at being approved to returning to take care of myself, or even to be with my parents. I am starting to fumble upon the concrete conclusion that I will never be able to leave. Even if I do, I'll be back."

My eyes sting with salty tears. Those poor men, their poor families, poor Randall. It was pitiful for all involved. His story led to one of those blank moments. When your mind is void of thoughts because the subject at hand is beyond comprehension. I want to scream in an outburst of sheer disillusionment that this story is capable of being so many people's reality.

"You're a really good person, Randal, genuinely. What happened to you, it breaks my heart, but you have to know it was not your fault. You did what you could." I promise Randall, after spending a moment consumed with shock.

"It felt nice to tell somebody without a Ph.D." He says emotionlessly, obviously talking about his story had evoked a silencing level of grief within him. We sit there for a moment, listening to the creek that runs behind Maze; the water makes a slight crackling sound as it glides over rock.

"Guilt makes you edible," Randall whispers.

"I think it makes you wither." I murmur, thinking about the last time I spoke with my dead sister and the ashy pallor of her corpse.

"I think we should go inside." He concludes.

"Yeah," I agree and pull myself into a standing position. I extend a hand, which Randall accepts. I walk him back to his room, us both in a quiet state of thoughtful reflection.

"Have a good night, June." Randall bids me farewell while opening his door.

"You too, Randall. Thank you so much for trusting me." I say, earnestly. He responds with a slight smile.

The second his door closes, I rip out my mobile and dial Addison. I slide down the hallway wall and wait for her to pick up. She does on the third ring. Before she can get out "hello," I have said "I love you" four times.

Randall's disturbing story had made me want to call my oldest sister. His experience, being horrendous beyond comprehension, is heartbreaking because Randall is so kind. That kindness reminds me of Addison. More though, it reminds me of how much Addison helped me when I, like Randall, was consumed by darkness.

Addison is the reason I got mental help when I was fourteen. When Elizabeth died, Addison, who was five months pregnant, moved home. At first, she slept in Lizzie's room which sent a chill down my spine with every passing night. It was heartbreaking. Through the thin walls, I would hear her sobbing at 3 AM, immersed in the scent of Lizzie's pillow. Cinnamon sugar, Elizabeth always smelt like a pan of my mom's cinnamon toast. Eventually, Addison transitioned to sleeping with me, in my bed.

It was rough at the beginning because Addison

was going through a violent round of morning sickness. A couple of times, she did not make it to the restroom or bedside trash can. I had the pleasure of waking up to the scent of hot vomit seeping into the carpet. Once she felt better, it was really nice. I like sleeping with my siblings. It brings me comfort. I still miss her presence some nights.

After Lizzie was buried, the night terrors tried to kill me. I would wake up, sure Elizabeth was beside me, but I would still be trapped in sleep. Then, when I felt like I was losing paralysis, and could finally roll over and see her, my ear-drums would be vibrated, almost to the point of bursting, by distinct screeching. I would wake up hysterical.

Worse than these dreams were the ones of us making fresh memories. I would dream of a day we had spent together. A day I must've forgotten. I would be so thankful that I had gotten to spend extra time with Lizzie before she died. Until I woke up and realized it was a façade. I could not go back and reverse missed opportunities to hang out. Our interactions were solidified. I woke up from these inconsolable.

These instances kept me from sleeping, as they would anybody. Not sleeping made me...itch. Except the itching was not on the surface. It was deep down, festering in my veins. I dug my finger-tips in brutally, scratching my skin to a shredded pulp. Honestly, I think I wanted to just pry the skin off because I could not stand to be in it anymore. It was a worn shell that I wanted to shed.

My sister was dead, my brother was leaving, and all I could do was pick at my flesh. It was like my reasonings and rationalities had evaporated from my troubled mind. I was in a state of inhuman craze. One day, after waking up soaked in sweat from a horrendous dream, I curled up into a ball in the corner of my room. I scratched at my face until blood leaked down my fingers and dried beneath my nail beds.

I remember looking into the mirror the next day and bawling my eyes out at my maimed reflection. I looked like a meth addict. Honestly, I swear, I was not doing the scratching on purpose. I can remember it, however, when it was happening, I had no clue that I was partaking in this self-mutilation. It was an outlandish, all-consuming, habit that reeked of deliriousness.

Addison immediately saw through the makeup I had slathered on. I was attempting to conceal the marks, but they were thick and fresh. The foundation mingled with the wounds creating clumpy, burgundy patches to form across my face. I looked like a hornet-nest victim. She took me to the doctor and after many, way too personal, talks I was prescribed Xanax. Was I thankful to be taking a narcotic at 14? *Honestly yes, because I could finally get some damn sleep.*

If it was not for Addison, I could have been checked into a juvenile facility for mental illness. Or worse, I could have been confined like poor Randall. Lord knows my mother would not have intervened. She already had a dead daughter; she did not need a crazy one too. My sister saved me. Jamie was more than right. I was cruel to have been ignoring her.

# CHAPTER TWELVE: UNHIGNED

I feel the need to defend Randall. He is brilliantly generous through thoughtful words. He expresses deep understanding thorough empathy. Dr. Brooks is not so great. He suppresses Randall. In fact, I am starting to see a correlation between him and subdue amongst all of the patients, or at least the three I am permitted to shadow. He makes them feel as if it is their fault they are struggling. That is the number one thing a Doctor of Psychology should never do. His behavior repulses me to the point of nausea.

The first time Dr. Brooks and I really got into it was surprisingly over my least favorite patient, Glinda. It happened two weeks into the program. I thought I picked up on something extremely helpful during one of her sessions. I was not belittling Dr. Brooks for not noticing the same thing. I am a respectful young lady, *verbally*. I was simply trying to share what I thought could be a factor in Glinda's convoluted psyche.

Dr. Brooks had asked Glinda who she would say had raised her. First, she said her mom and dad. Then casually added, "oh and daycare."

Dr. Brooks just skipped over that information like he was scanning an online Terms & Agreements contract. He continued. "So, you give your mother and father that credit?"

I assumed he had an intricate idea that he was trying to extract from her mind by talking about her parents. The conversation ended up being lackluster. I came to the conclusion that, perhaps, he had not heard her mention daycare.

After she had left, I approached. At first, I was even excited to discuss it with him. This is the career I plan to pursue. Any psychologist is an inspiration, or so I thought.

"Dr. Brooks?" His dull-grey eyes stayed glued to a sheet he was checking off. I clear my throat and persevere. "I noticed Glinda had mentioned daycare. I know that affects some people negatively. Do you think that could have been something that set her illness into motion?"

Dr. Brooks continues to reserve his gaze for the paper and not me. "Uh, probably not."

I was completely thrown off guard by his nonchalant response. I continued to try and explain, more confused than upset at this point. "Well it's just, she obviously has attention starvation issues. Even to the point of insanity. Is it possible her alters could be imaginary friends? People that she fabricated when stranded in a place without her family and, possibly, without friends?"

This time Dr. Brooks does look at me before responding, his stare stone cold. "I went to daycare, Miss Wilson. Are you saying I also think I am Dr. Mustard and Dr. Horseradish? Saying that I too have multiple personalities because of it?" Oh, my goodness. He would want his other two personalities to still be doctors. I bit my tongue before it asked if his fourth one was Dr. Fuckface.

I tried to salvage the situation because I had no desire to be on bad terms with anyone here. I certainly am not implying that every child who attends daycare is mentally ill. I understand that parents have other obligations. Plus, nowadays daycare facilities seem much nicer. But when I began kindergarten, I realized that certain kids were always striving to be a bold presence in their teacher's or classmates' daily routines.

When I asked my mother why in the world kids would act like that, she would acknowledge that the kids were obnoxious and immature. She would also say, "it really is sad." She never elaborated on what she meant. At the time, I did not give her words much thought.

It was not until I was in fourth grade that I understood and was overcome by a similar sense of dejection. A certain group of children, many being the overbearing ones, would always depart in a white van after school. *Not a candy-induced mass abduction.* It was a van taking them to their daycare center.

One day my mother was driving me home from school, but there was a roadblock; we ended up going a different way. This alternate route caused us to pass the aforementioned daycare. As we drove by, I saw dingy toys crowded in a corner of the minuscule backyard, a half-caved in trampoline, and a pencil-thin, scar-ridden woman smoking a cigarette. She was wearing a stained polo and sported a teddy bear shaped name tag. As we drove around the front, my widened eyes landed on a large group of children, many being my classmates, eating what seemed to be cheese sandwiches at dilapidated picnic tables. Those kids were not yelling or drawing attention to themselves like usual. They were just sitting there like zombies, feeling what their brains would later process as a complicated mixture of disappointment and resentment.

In an effort in reassuring myself that it could not be that bad, I asked my mom how long they could be there. I was assuming it could not be for more than a few hours at a time. She informed me that when she was in high school, she spent a summer working at a similar facility. She said that people would drop off their children as early as 5:00 AM and pick them up as late as 10:00 PM. She added that it was not just kids my age that went, younger children, even newborns stayed there. I sat in my booster seat feeling about as much sorrow as my little body could. The entire experience traumatized me, and I did not even attend.

Dr. Brooks did not need to know this whole story, but to me it made sense. In a more simplified manner, I tried to reason with him. "Oh no! I am not saying it is wrong to send your children to daycare, or that if you do they will struggle. I just mean some parents abuse it, leaving their kids there all day every day, and then do not give them attention at home. If a child has friends then I am sure they don't mind it, but if not, it could be hard for a kid to find company. They may have to come up with their own. That's why I feel like daycare could be relevant to Glinda."

"Well Miss Wilson, my son is at daycare right now. Want to go pick him up? I'm sure you would be a better nanny than you are an intern," said Dr. Brooks in a tone that challenged me. I felt my heart sink as my blood boiled. All I could do was walk out before I burst into angry tears.

That incident was just the start. If Dr. Brooks wanted to belittle me, whatever. He could try his darndest. It is when I see his treatment of Randall that I cannot keep my mouth shut, and my thoughts reserved.

I am sitting in on one of Randall's sessions as is routine for Thursday mornings. The doctor half-attempts to get Randall to unlatch his feelings, as per usual. This process is incredibly redundant. Randall is an open book. He expresses every last thought to Dr. Brooks. The issue is that Dr. Brooks has no clue how to address these complex emotions. He compensates by continuously encouraging Randall to dig deeper.

This poorly thought out coaxing shoves the session down a steep hill. Randall only becomes increasingly distraught until reaching an incoherent state. He is then ushered off by some experienced orderly.

After hearing Randall confess the horror story

that led him to Maze, I am a million times more agitated with Dr. Brooks. It is five weeks into the program, and a week after Randall admitted to me the source of his PTSD. I am done indulging Dr. Brooks. Randall is a defenseless patient who deserves adequate, if not excellent, care.

I go to visit Randall a couple of hours after his session. I inquire on his state of well-being. He supplies me with the most pitiful answer. "I just want to go home."

I feel my lungs become weighted. I do not care if it is inappropriate to touch the patients. *Wait, not like that. Not about to blow this twenty-seven-year-old, don't worry.* I tread to where Randall is sitting on his bed, studying the linoleum floor. I wrap my arms around him tightly. He begins to weep softly.

"I'm getting better June, but they won't let me leave. Nurses, orderlies, other patients, they all say to me that I'll get out soon. That I am doing so well." This is true; that is his reputation. Everybody advocates that Randall is ready for discharge.

"Then every few weeks, the government psychologists come and talk to me for no more than thirty minutes. They say no. He is very ill. He must stay. I know stuff June, secrets. I know locations. I know how it was when we were over there. One day, it's going to come out. There is something not right in the White House, in Iraq. It is so damn convoluted and corrupt." He lifts his trembling fingers up to fidget with his torn ear.

"But I would never tell! That's the government and their corruption. I respect the military. I took an oath, and that's that. Yet, I have a history of mental illness and suffer from PTSD. The goblins running this country from the sidelines, they don't trust people like me, and they never will. They may not supply us with all the facts, but they sure do have a way of keeping us prisoners of war."

My knee shakes as my mind tries to reject the unsettling truth that Randall is sputtering. I do not live under a rock, I realize that things have been messy since 9/11. That the government may be abusing the military. I remember that African American congressman, or something political, Powell maybe? Anyway, the one who gave the anthrax speech, before we declared war with Iraq. I know his lack of validity and ensuing resignation did not sit right with my parents or my brother. But I never paid it that much mind. My sister was killed three months before the towers were hit. She died in June. The tragedy and its resulting craze was a blur for a fourteen-year-old girl, broken-hearted and on the brink of puberty. *I just knew I would never read my kids, My Pet Goat.*

Honestly, Randall's life should be the plot of a highly disturbing film. A sane enough man, a veteran for Christ's sakes, being held hostage in an asylum. This Hell is Randall's reality. All I can do is reassure him that he will get out one day, even though my words are without substance.

"You know what one of the hardest parts is, June?" Randall asks, his swollen eyes pleading.

"What?" I blink rapidly to keep my own eyes from spilling.

"The fact that doctors are allowed to minimize me while I am trapped here. If they won't let me leave, could they at least get me some help? Make my thoughts manageable, give me something to live for." That's when I know what I have to do. I am officially pursuing Dr. Brook's termination. I cannot intervene with the government, but I can ease some of Randall's agony, or at least try to.

I leave his room riddled with sickening nerves. I must seek help in this situation. I feel a juvenile sense of awkward timidity. I have to start with Lacey because she is my supervisor. Lacey is in the dark about what has been going on. Nurses seldom listen in on patient's sessions.

The morning after my upsetting talk with Randall, I decide to tell her over breakfast. Lacey's reaction is priceless.

"Me oh my! I'm going to rabble-rouse like this place has never seen. I'll give Brooksy a good enough smack to send him to a physical hospital, that's what I'll do." Blood pools in my mouth as teeth pierce my tongue in an attempt to prevent giggling at the phrase "physical hospital."

"June, we are going to the front office. Grab your cup, darlin'." Instructs a fired-up Lacey as she stands up so fast, I feel a head rush for her.

"What are we doing Lacey?" I ask, suddenly feeling out of the loop.

"We are complaining sweetie. I ain't playing his games." She responds, her eyes zeroing in on the stairs like a target.

When we get to the front office, Lacey requests Michael. We are informed that he has taken a personal day. This means we have to settle for the orangutan looking woman, Miranda, that was so unwelcoming on my first day at Maze. Either Lacey does not care for her either, or she is just livid with the situation because her tone is shrill, and her directions precise.

"Miranda, June is filing a complaint to the director about Dr. Brooks. She will tell you the first-hand experience. I will sign as her supervisor." Miranda seems neutral to the situation. She rolls her eyes while asking me to come to her side of the computer she is lazily typing on.

Miranda pulls up an email box. In the subject, she writes "Intern Complaint." She then spins in her swivel chair to look at me. "Go for it."

Oh, wow. I did not realize I would be writing the email word for word. Okay, time to be a big girl. Wait, what is the director's name again?

Luckily, Miranda has keen senses. By the way my fingers are hovering over the keyboard, she realizes that I am struggling. "Girl, it's Henry Maze the third. It's his grandson remember?" *Oh right.* Do I literally address somebody as a third?

I did. Here is a copy of the letter:

Dear Henry Maze III,

I am writing to you concerning Dr. Brooks, who is belittling the patients. My name is June Wilson, and I am a 2005 summer intern. Patients should not be talked down to and treated as if they are idiotic. No matter what their mental state may be. Ego should never block a professional's path.

The man displays excessive arrogance and thoughtlessness. His words are infused with a crude nature as if the patients were absurd for what they have confessed. I have caught him several times throwing out loaded words that give the impression of intelligence but are not actually correlated with the topic being discussed.

Dr. Brooks is trying to perplex the patients. He is basically telling them they are what they think they are. Most of the time, this means they are worthless. It is starting to become unsettlingly apparent what a toll his words take on Maze's patients. When he speaks, they become hushed and squirm uncomfortably. It is upsetting to see them absorb such useless information. I know they must feel increasingly alone after each session. One example is patient Randall Creed, a respected military man. Dr. Brooks is especially rude and trivializing towards him. I do not think the military would be without action if Randall's inadequate treatment was brought to their attention.

I am advocating for the termination of Dr. Brooks from this facility. Thank you for taking my concerns into consideration.

Sincerely,
June Wilson

Was I being passive aggressive? Heck, yes. Did I use bold font? Indeed, I did. It is unacceptable for Dr. Brooks to be employed here, a *disgrace*. With every word written, my fury intensified. I have always been shy and easy to push over. Standing up for something in such a bold way makes me feel exceptional. I feel like growth is real, like you do get more confidence with age. I am basically a fine wine now.

Lacey reads my letter before typing her name under mine. At first, I am worried that she will find the message unprofessional and alter my words. Instead, I see her face glow like a freshly lit Christmas tree. She looks at me in disbelief and exclaims, "you're a feisty little momma, aren't you? I love it!"

I beam back at her, feeling like I could take on the world.

As we walk back upstairs, Lacey catches me off guard with a personal question. "So hun, how are things with you and Evan? I see y'all holding hands in the hallway. Sweeter than my mama's cornbread!" Okay, Evan and I have a stalker. *Good to know.*

Now Evan, Evan Carter. *You might want to skip ahead if you want to avoid reading a couple pages of how two quirky teens fell into like within the walls of an asylum.* I am going to keep it brief, but I am going to gush because every girl deserves to talk about her first real crush. Over the past few weeks, we have gone on some more dates. I have avoided sharing because it is indulgent, but hey one story can't hurt. I think part of growing up might just be realizing that it's okay to release more than the serious and the morose.

Our relationship has been warming up significantly since our first night together. Pretty sure it's close to boiling at this point. The closeness started to escalate when we made some… poor choices. T'was the night after Jamie's visit. I was mopey the rest of the day, so Evan decided to take action.

He had brought a little bit, a whole bottle, of Jack with him to Maze. Why? No clue. Maybe he just wanted to drink by himself. Maybe since he never had siblings it was his way to cope with loneliness. Or he just brought it because he is 18 and teenagers feel powerful when they have alcohol, whether they drink it or not, whichever way, I do not blame him. The only times I have gotten drunk were with my cat, and it was absolutely to fill a vacant void in my life. Unfortunately, scotch stolen from under your mom's bed is not really a substitute for your dead sister or unstable family, *who knew.*

When he asked me if I was down to drink, I agreed. I warned I may suck at it. I might puke all over him and/or go on a rant about fascism. Yet, he was still game. So, the plan was to go to town, grab a meat-lovers pizza, pick-up lemon-lime soda (we are 18, do not judge), and buy some plastic cups. Unfortunately, we got caught up, making out on my bed for too long. By the time we left Maze, it was 10 o'clock at night. I do not know if you remember that Maze locks at 10:30, but we certainly did not.

"Evan, should we like a break a window or something?" I asked as we sat in his running rental car, panicking. Yet not freaking out enough to refrain from chowing down on God's cheesy gift to humanity.

"Uhhhh no, Juney. I think we can handle a night in the car." He assured, his full lips shiny with pizza grease.

"But what if we die from carbon monoxide poisoning?" I blurted out.

Evan chuckled. "Well, that would be an unfortunate call to our parents. What if we just get drunk?"

"Yeah, I guess that would be the adult thing to do." I agreed. We started pouring shots into the frail cups and downing them quickly. My throat burned, but I had no desire to add the mixer. I wanted the unwinding effect without extenuating the smolder. Once we were feeling on the goofy side, we reclined our seats to face each other as we chattered away. I swear being drunk brings your voice up to full volume and increases the speed of your jibber-jabber to that of light. Finally, we settled down enough to have a, *somewhat,* coherent conversation.

"You remind me of coffee, June." Evan tried to whisper in a tone that is anything but hushed.

"What?!" I asked animatedly.

"Or like… you're like a cappuccino." He clarified.

"Um. Pardon?" I begged.

"Like I don't get how people drink plain coffee. It doesn't make sense. But most people are plain coffee because they are boring and bitter, and they hardly make sense. You are so sweet and purposeful. Like caffeinated steamed milk, with a little bean-water for energy. Like you should be drunk." He slurred.

"I am drunk, Evan." I laughed. His statement was a loose metaphor, but it was sweet nonetheless.

"No, No, June, that's not what I mean. Like I think about you allllll the time. The other day, Thomas, the car wreck guy, had a snap. He told me that when I grow up, he is going to track me down, come to my home, and burn it to the ground. Even if my wife and children are inside. He said he actually hopes they are, but all I could think was, *I wonder how June likes her eggs*." His speech became compromised by delirious snickers. My heart began to flutter, *even though I hate eggs.*

"Evan!" drunk June replies excitedly. "I understand a few days ago, Pearl had a meltdown, realizing her husband was never coming back for her, and I was thinking, *I bet Evan looks cute in a flannel*."

"We are horribleeee people, Juney-E." He covers his face.

"Speak for yourself. I ain't killed nobody, Evan-C. I'm a good girl." I stammer. "And also, you smell like my favorite fabric softener."

Evan parts his hands to reveal his flushed face. "I like you so much, girl."

"I like you more than that guy banned from the craft room likes to eat chalk," I inform him.

Smitten, psychotic kittens. Here's the thing, I have no girlfriends and Lizzie is gone, so I am thrilled for Lacey to ask about him. I cannot share with her that particular story, probably would get kicked out of the program it being illegal and all but having the opportunity to gab about him feels freeing. Poor Lacey does not know she just turned over a full pitcher of sweet tea.

"Lacey, we have so much in common! I feel like I just made him in a machine or wrote him into a novel, but like, with added qualities I did not know existed. He is a huge fan of 70's music, we both adore horror, and he even has a dark sense of humor that revels mine at times. I'm sure you have noticed, I'm a quiet girl. I usually need extensive time to warm-up. I can talk to Evan effortlessly. We have such similar life philosophies, he's just so chill about it. About everything! He's the most relaxed person I have ever met. I find his presence to be so calming." I blurt all of this out, overlapping my words, a toothy grin glued to my face the entire time I am speaking. *Geez, could I be more of a teenage girl? Oh wait, it's cool. I am one.*

"Oh, my goodness!! Girly, that's fantastical! I swear from the moment I introduced you two, I just knew y'all were destined to fall in love. Like some kind of psychosis sense or something." *Psychic*? "I just knew it!" Exclaims Lacey.

Then her tone proceeds to soften like lotioned hands. Her amused smile transitions to a cheeky smirk. "So, have y'all shook boots yet?" She asks as her bony elbow nudges my ribcage.

*Awkward.* I feel my face flush with blotchy color, a customary reaction. Why in the world would she ask something like that? I uncomfortably grind my mental gears trying to think of a response.

My words fumble as I tell her the truth.

"I don't really… put out." I admit, the hue of red, sprouting beneath my skin, darkens a shade.

Lacey stares at me, her left eyebrow raised. Obviously, a little puzzled by my bluntness. She was either expecting me to say yes, or that I was waiting for marriage, or something special. She gathers herself before responding, "well good for you June. Respect is a virtue."

I cannot leave the conversation so stale. Guilt will gnaw at me, plus that was a very vague truth. I owe her an elaboration.

"It's not that I plan on never having sex. It's just not something I have done before so, I don't really know what's going to happen. I don't even know… like what I would do… like I don't even know how it is supposed to be touched." I tell Lacey, staggering over the last confession.

She throws her head back while omitting a slew of bubbly chuckles. When her brown eyes meet mine again, her cheerful demeanor resumes. "Oh sweetie, you will find out. Trust me, they like it touched in any form or fashion."

At this point, I am following her as she flutters around bed-ridden patients like a hyper hummingbird. "And I mean once you do it, you can find what y'all both like. For example, my hubby and I, we do a lot of role-playing."

"Uh Lacey," I whisper, realizing the liver-spot covered man she is checking vitals on is very much lucid, he moans, she ignores.

"Maze is a great inspiration. Sometimes, after work, I'll just keep on my scrubs, and he'll lay in the bed. I am a sexy nurse, and he is a patient who only has one more bang left in him. I mean obviously, I haven't showered or anything so there are still bodily fluids on me, which I know sounds gross; but he likes me to be a dirty girl."

"Lacey..." I murmur again.

"Other times, we are two lunatics, who have just escaped the asylum together." *Aww like when Evan and I pretended to be runaways.* "But we like really commit to the crazy charade. He will drool and slap himself. Plus, he's perfected this creepy cackle. Here I'll do it for you—"

"Lacey!" I interject. *This woman is out of her mind.*

From my suggestive head tilt, she finally catches my drift. "Oh sorry, Mr. Davis." She says sheepishly, still giggling.

Lacey begins changing an IV bag, then she seems to come up with a grand idea. Lacey turns to me with an open mouth. Her eyes gleam with animation as she claps and bounces on her pedicured toes. Syrupy fluid leaks from the bag she is clutching. Lacey could not care less if her scrubs are now spotted with questionable substances. She is engrossed in her idea. Plus, apparently, Lacey and her husband enjoy shacking up in others' filth anyway.

Wow, I think I even see a legit light bulb hovering above her head. *Ding.*

"Juney, Juney, Juney I have a fabulous idea! You, me, Evan, and my hubby should go out Saturday night! There is this amazing little place we go to every week. Y'all will love it!" She half-shouts. Giving Mr. Davis a startle that could very well end his already brittle life.

There is no way I could ever reject Lacey's invitation. It would crush her like a fallen elevator. Why would I say no anyway? I am desperate to get out. I am going a tad nuts myself. I am also curious to meet her husband.

"Let's do it!" I agree with anxious excitement.

"Joy!" Lacey skips over to give a mini, hug. *Wash your hands girlfriend.* "So, Saturday, 7?"

"It's a date," I assure.

"A double one!!" She cries, finally leaving Mr. Davis so the poor man may rest in peace. *Hopefully, while alive.*

# CHAPTER THIRTEEN: CRAZY

Saturday comes quicker than necessary. *Why you trying to rush me, week?* The night is now upon me and getting dressed is a challenge. For the most part, I have been wearing scrubs for the past five weeks. I also have not been super on top of my makeup since Evan has already witnessed morning June. *God bless his soul.*

I need to look perfect tonight. I let the bathroom brim with billowy steam as I take an extended shower. I have to shampoo my hair, repeat, condition my hair, repeat, shave my legs, exfoliate, wash, and then exfoliate a little more with a sugar scrub that is most-likely expired. After my lengthy rinse, I slather on a gallon of "soothing" lotion to counteract the scaly skin caused by the glide of my razor. I blow dry my hair carefully, using a styling brush, just like Lizzie taught me when I was twelve. My copper colored hair comes out surprisingly smooth like silky satin. Once I iron it, my locks are void of frizz.

I concentrate on my makeup with the intensity and precision of an Olympic athlete. I steady myself and refrain from rushing like usual. I also do not attempt multitasking and simultaneously brushing my teeth like most mornings. I even use an eyelash curler, or at least I think that's what this contraption is. It was in my Christmas stocking one year. I held on to it because my older sisters already had one and did not want it.

I choose a light-weight slip dress that I do not recall packing. My closet was a catastrophe at home, so it was probably bound-by-static-cling to something else I threw into my suitcase. Boy was it convenient to have, that's why messy girls are more... prepared? *Okay, we pretty much suck. This is purely an exception.*

The dress is pale pink, closer to neutral than cotton candy color. It is straight but a bit flowy. It is suspended from my shoulders by flimsy spaghetti straps, so thin they could be considered angel hair. When I was sixteen, I got the gown as a hand me down from Elizabeth. At the time, I thought it made me look frumpy. By now, my B's have morphed into C's. The baby fat that once insulated my cheeks has been trimmed, and my legs have elongated substantially. I am not a knockout, never will be. I will always have the girl-next-door look, but I am perfectly secure in that. I look elegant, almost as pretty as my sister had when she wore it on her first date with her last boyfriend.

Evan knocks on my door fifteen minutes before Lacey and her husband are set to pick us up. He looks adorable in a casual butter-yellow button down that makes his sun-kissed skin glow.

"Juney-E you look gorgeous." He breathes while falling back in mock shock. We both giggle as I playfully push on his chest.

Evan leans in to kiss me, but right before his lips meet mine, he asks, "has anyone ever told you your eyes look like swimming pools?"

After accepting the oddest compliment, I have ever received, Evan and I walk downstairs and breeze out of our asylum. He is telling me that a bunch of his friends are having a big graduation party tonight.

"I'm sad that I am not sad, you know? In the past, I would have been siked for a bash like this, but now all I can think of is how ridiculous they are for their over-the-top get-togethers," Evan says, seemingly annoyed. "I went into high school having friends that I had known since kindergarten. I graduated high school knowing that they are all immature jerks who only want to do bumps and take advantage of girls who are too drunk to even spell consent, much less give it. I want nothing to do with them. How can that be, how can people get so shitty?" He inquires.

"Evan I never had friends," I say flatly. *Honesty is the best policy.*

Lacey's car pulls up just in time to save me from his response. "Hi angels! Oh, my goodness gracious. I am downright thrilled to see you guys. My favorite couple ever!" is Lacey's greeting. Does she even prefer us as a couple over her parents? *Is she already drunk?*

133

Upon arriving at a restaurant called "Harold's," I realize Lacey's version of an intimate eatery is a sports bar. The moment we are seated, Lacey begins to jibber jabber at a nonstop rate. We get her whole story before receiving our entrees. Surprisingly, Lacey has a somewhat dark past.

"So yeah, I worked at a psychiatric hospital in Tennessee. It was a good time, little too good of a time. If you know what I mean." *I really don't.* "I just got too involved with one of my favorite patients," Lacey admits this with no hesitation or shame. I love that she specifies "one" of her favorite patients.

The patient she mentions is now sitting directly across from me drinking a stout. Mason, not the jar, is Lacey's husband. We had gotten his back story too. That was pre-appetizer entertainment.

"Mason was the victim of a joke gone wrong." Lacey had explained. "You know how boys are! Mason and his hunting buddies were on a retreat, and he had a few too many lagers. They are his kryptonite. That's why he ain't having any tonight." Lacey had laughed, genuinely. *Yeah, most stouts are only 10% alcohol content, you sure showed him.*

"Anywho, he played this little, insignificant joke where he cut up his hunting buddies' fishing licenses and made 'em sample a handful of raw deer meat. He supervised, and well this is the part that was a little distasteful, while he was watching them, he held a double barrel shotgun to their heads." *Uhhhh okay, quick escalation.*

"But!" Lacey added defensively, probably in response to mine and Evan's horrified expressions.

"My Mason is harmless. He is just a good old-fashioned redneck with some bizarre" *possibly lethal* "quirks."

"So, I promise the romantic part is coming y'all stay with me. After that incident, one of the guys confessed it to his wife, totally unnecessary. She was extraordinarily unsettled and angry, to say the least. Mason tried to assure her of the truth. That it was just guy stuff. The drama queen thought otherwise, though. Later that night, Mason heard the police pull up. Poor thing was just chilling, playing video games in his boxers. So then, he was checked into where I worked. His high school sweetheart, fair-weather whore, left him after he was dubbed insane. They only locked him in a mental ward for six weeks. I mean c'mon."

So, after Lacey had provided us with this startling information overload, food had intervened. Now she is resuming her story.

"Anyway, let me go back and explain how Mason and I started to fall in love. I had just graduated from nursing school a few weeks prior to his incident. The hospital was one of my clinical sites, so heck yeah, I accepted a job there! I adored the asylum atmosphere, obviously, I still do. I feel like I really benefit from being both a physical and mental healer." She pauses. We smile and nod.

"I met Mason, oh goodness you kids are going to love this." *Will we though?* "I first saw him the exact day his ex-fiancée came to officially say her goodbyes. How perfect is that? Anyway, my firecracker over here, he punched a wall that day." She stops for emphasis.

"Baby cracked up his knuckles completely. It was beyond pitiful. I helped treat the darlin,' and he got to telling me what had happened. I felt so much empathy for him, bless his heart. We just stuck like PB&J." *Guess you could say it was love at first bandage?*

"Then, we just started spending bushels of time together. I, silly me, used that big mouth of mine and told a few of the nurses. This one old bat," I can see Lacey is gritting her teeth, "she was so wrinkly and bitter. She went and told everybody, including my supervisors." I do not believe in tattle-tailing either but, dang Lacey, let the man heal.

"Now, I don't think they would have even paid her story much mind. I was kinda the crowd favorite there." She actually says the next part with hints of guilt and disdain in her now quiet tone. "Unfortunately, there ended up also being some security cam footage of me sneaking in to… well give Mason an extra dose of medicine, if ya know what I mean." *We all do, Lacey.*

"They weren't even going to fire me though! My head-supervisor confronted me. He said if I would give up Mason, then I could stay. No probation, it would all be in the past. I like to think that is because I am just that good at my job, but I have a feeling not many other nurses want the glamor of working in a mental institution." She snickers and slaps her knee at her joke that was not quite a joke.

"I told those folks look, I never plan to stop loving my Mason as long as I live. I will give out a holler to any and every institution and find myself a better job because he is my big, strong buck, and I his dainty doe." As Lacey concludes her story, she looks at her husband with a tender gaze of admiration. Mason continues to only pay attention to the football game on the TV above the bar, which he has been doing the entire meal. I actually think he is a mute, or constantly puts himself on it so that Lacey may have the floor.

She giggles in utter bliss before planting a sloppy kiss on his unnoticing cheek. "So y'all babies aren't the only ones to find love in an asylum!"

Evan and I both stare back at the woman, our eyes widened to the size of sand dollars. I feel his grip tighten around mine as we both realize perhaps you do have to be a bit unwell to work at Maze. I put every ounce of energy I have into stifling a chuckle as Evan's foot softly kicks my ankle.

I will admit, the conversation at dinner is only kept from an unbearably awkward fate due to Lacey's talkative disposition. Quite frankly, I think this is her chance to finally get out some chatter that must have been bottling up. She speaks as if somebody is paying her a $100 per word. *A job I would go broke doing.*

By the time the waiter offers dessert, I am about ready to slice off my ears and offer them to her in surrender. Of course, she says she would love some and selects the heftiest piece of cookies and cream cheesecake known to man. It puts my slender slice of key lime pie to absolute shame.

I expect her to continue on her rant, now focused on saving the butterflies instead of the bees, but am surprised when she turns the subject towards me and Evan. "So, lovebirds, when are y'all meeting the folks?"

Her question makes me feel winded, as if I have suffered a hard fall. I would have suspected her to ask how we were going to make it work long distance. Maybe even if we had dropped the L-bomb yet. We have not *by the way.*

The parent is a leap, a bound. Evan makes the first move by coolly saying, "that's a great question, Lacey! I've been thinking, maybe I should follow you home after Maze ends Juney. Spend a day or two in your hometown. Meet some friends, family, wouldn't that be fun?" He looks at me eagerly.

It is clear from his gleaming eyes that he genuinely wants this to happen. He is not simply trying to appease Lacey in an answer. My body immediately stiffens like the beginning effects of rigor mortis is setting in. Evan does not need to meet my family. I want to spare him that uncomfortable introduction, and honestly, I need to continue keeping him in the dark about Elizabeth.

Is this selfish? *Possibly.* Am I going to feel guilty about it? *Probably.* Will I change my mind? *Absolutely not.* I loathe the heaviness of Elizabeth. *Not calling my dead sister fat.*

It's just, it weirds people out. After Elizabeth was killed, people acted differently towards me, not in the way that they were kinder. It was not like in movies, where death evokes empathy. No, the people I shared my high school's halls with were gossipy and snarky about it. She died at the beginning of the summer, between my last year of middle and first year of high school. I wish my parents would have transferred me or kept me home.

The subject of her accident seemed to be the hot topic of the summer, and everyone seemed to have an opinion about it. One that they decided to voice loudly anytime I was in earshot. They knew I was timid and would never say anything, just look down in hurt defeat. I guess it was a cheap thrill for fifteen-year-old girls, to me it was just cruel.

I heard things like "her sister was a whore; her reputation was dead long before she actually croaked" or "guess that's what ya get for drinking a bottle of jack by yourself, not only your kidneys drown." I even heard a couple older guys say, "sucks the little sister isn't as hot as Lizzie. Maybe one of us can at least teach her how to blow as good."

Not really phrases that helped me to heal. That's who Jamie was referring to. He had seen the girl, who made the kidney joke, at the grocery store.

I would never think for a millisecond that Evan would ever act crude to me about her death in any form or fashion. On the contrary, I cringe at the thought of how understanding yet saddened he would be. It is apparent in his gentle touch and sweet words that he truly cares for me. Finding out something so tragic about my family would definitely upset him. Whatever reaction it induces, Lizzie's story always muddles things to an irreversible point. It alters perceptions of me and my family. My eyes dampen at the thought of Evan looking at me any differently.

At the current moment, it would be inappropriate and flat out mean to deny Evan his want. Instead of answering, I simply smile and place a peck on his soft cheek. I then take a huge swig of my ice water, wishing with my whole heart that it was vodka.

# CHAPTER FOURTEEN: WILD

"Did you like hate her or something?" Victoria asks abruptly as we try to help Pearl stitch her new quilt during arts and crafts time. The Friday after my double date from Hell, I am exhausted. It has been a long and trivializing week. Noelle has the stomach flu, so Victoria has been with me and Lacey the entire week. *Gag me with a fucking spoon.*

Victoria has not humbled. I have just learned how to alter my daily routine to avoid run-ins with the spoiled brat. If anything, Victoria has actually evolved into more of a vicious snake after the first time she saw Evan place a soft kiss atop my head before we walked into the cafeteria. Still, this week we have had to tolerate each other more than usual. You would think she would be mature enough to handle that but *nope*.

"Who?" I inquire, perplexed.

"Your sister," she replies, not even looking up

from her needlework.

I am stunned. How does she know about Elizabeth? How did she get to such a drastic assumption? Has she told anybody else? Has she told Evan?

Victoria seems to misread my hesitation and confusion as curiosity and continues to speak. "I read your admission essay, June. Told Michael you said it was fine. That I was trying to write a college paper and needed some inspiration. He is such a freaking push-over." *Is this really happening? Is that legal?*

"Anyway," Victoria keeps on, still not lifting her eyes. "You talk about how her death shaped you, and all this stuff. But I have never heard you talk about her. So, what? Did you guys not get along?"

I am immersed in mystified disbelief. Goodness gracious is this girl bold. Literally, her admitting all that information can get her purged from the program. Victoria knows that if I tell anybody, it will be her word against mine. As much as I want to violently yank her ebony hair out and send her on her merry way back to the peach state, that is not worth pursuing.

Seriously though, where did she muster such nerve? Plus, to say it in front of Pearl, who can under no circumstances vouch for me because of sanity, but is still a person with working ears. Well, actually from taking another look at Pearl, and the line of drool oozing from the corner of her mouth, maybe I cannot give Victoria that much ballsy credit.

I have no earthly clue how to respond but I know arguing ethics will be a waste of time. So, instead, I actually decide to go in for an answer. "Of course not. I loved my sister. It's just a lot to talk about." I say, hoping to shut her up.

I am unsuccessful. "Yeah, but according to my psychological research, most people with true grief want to talk about that person. Either because they can't get that person off their minds, or they want to honor them," she continues, looking up for the first time. Her glance is brief.

"Well, I guess I'm past grief then," I respond, meaning it.

"When did she die?" Victoria asks.

"Four years ago," I offer, not thinking twice about it.

"Mhm and how long did it take you to not want to speak about her?" She queries.

"I don't know, not that long," I answer, starting to be pushed towards the edge of my mental chair.

"How'd she die?" Victoria prods, once again not lifting her satisfied head.

*That was enough.* "None of your freaking business, Victoria! Are you seriously trying to shrink me right now?" I stand up and yank the quilt from her pale hands. Her needle shatters against the hard floor. I storm away, leaving poor Pearl shook up, and nasty Victoria a little embarrassed for once. *Why couldn't she just be alive still.*

I called her a bitch, not Victoria, Elizabeth. When I was fourteen, I had these gorgeous pearl earrings. They were real, fathered by the ocean. The pearls were silky, their complexion shimmered with a subtle rose undertone. They made me look elegant and sophisticated, made my smile gleam. My parents rarely got me anything special growing up. I was the queen of hand me downs, but that Christmas they got me those earrings.

I never minded sharing with my sisters, but those pearls were different. I adored them, and Elizabeth was notorious for losing things, especially jewelry. She was not overprotective like Addison or grounded like me. She could be extremely ditzy. Often times misplacing one of her slippers or breaking the charms from her bracelets. My mother had to drive back to many stores because Elizabeth had left her purse behind. Still, I usually let her borrow my things, however, those pearl studs were mine.

My sister wore these gaudy chandelier earrings on the day of her graduation. She felt they brought out the gold accents in her dress and exemplified the darker hues in her hair. They looked fine on her. Not the most flattering I had seen, but they were good enough.

That night, her and two of her friends came to the house to get ready before going to their big party. As I was walking up the stairs and into my room, a bowl of popcorn in one hand, my cat in the other, I caught Elizabeth standing over my dresser. I set both of my loves down on my bed and came up behind her.

She did not even turn to look at me. Instead, she stared into the small mirror atop my vanity as she slipped something into her ear. "You don't mind if I wear these right, Juniper?"

The light bouncing off the pearls caught my eye in her reflection. I immediately felt my body tense. "Elizabeth! Those are my special ones. No, you seriously cannot."

She finally turned, her expression smug, not even phased by what I had just said. "Yes, I can, June. It's my graduation night. Don't you want it to be special for me?"

She really could be such a petty girl sometimes. "Elizabeth, you will lose them, or they will fall out. Y'all are going to be outside for crying out loud! Wear some knock-offs. Those are mine." I plead, becoming desperate.

"No, I want to look perfect tonight. They match my nice, ivory blouse. Seriously, I am wearing them, June. Consider it part of your graduation gift to me." She shot back as she began to walk into mine and Delilah's Jack and Jill style bathroom.

I grabbed her right shoulder to stop her, but she violently jerked out from my grasp. "You are literally such a bitch Elizabeth!" I yelled as she casually strode off. All she did in response was lift her middle finger at me.

My sister took her last breath while wearing those earrings, only a few hours later. Addison had provided the clothes for Elizabeth's corpse. She asked if I wanted my pearls back. I told her no. That I would rather Elizabeth be buried with a piece of me.

That was not necessarily the truth. I knew what was on her decaying body meant little in retrospect. I just wanted them out of my sight for good. Their presence haunted me. At the viewing, I almost vomited on her powdered skin when I saw them catch that signature glint of light. So, yeah, I called my sister a bitch. Not only were they my last words to her, but it was the last thing she ever heard me describe her as. All over a pair of earrings that will rot with her forever, no longer holding any value to me other than shame.

That memory replays, and consumes me, as I sit on my bed after the incident with Victoria, tears streaming. Victoria was in the wrong for asking, but sometimes I cannot help but feel mounds of resentment towards my ill-fated sister.

My thoughts are interrupted by a light knock on my door. I am flabbergasted to see an unfamiliar face when I open it. I was hoping for Evan. I would have blamed the tears on PMS.

"Hi, are you June?" asks a short, sturdy girl with wildly curly hair.

"Yes," I answer.

"Michael at the front office needs to see you." She states flatly before trotting off.

Oh no, I am in trouble. *Colossal trouble.* I should not have raised my voice at Victoria. I definitely should not have aggressively pulled the quilt from her. Oh God, hopefully I had not sent Pearl into a meltdown. My stomach fills with churning dread as I tread down the stairs and to the office area. I am being sent home. *I just know it.*

When I tiptoe into Michael's office, I can instantly tell that he is nervous, as he has been any other time I have seen him. The emotion basically wafts from the meek man. There does seem to be a promising sense of satisfaction in his tone, and expression, as he tells me to have a seat. I sit in the thin, flexible-backed chair facing his desk. I have no uncertainty that a petrified look is helplessly pasted to my face. My bottom lip quivers.

Michael begins to give me a speech he undoubtedly has rehearsed. "Well, Miss. Wilson, I want you to know that your allegations towards Dr. Wayne Brooks have been taken extremely seriously. You see, this is not the first complaint. He has been on occupational probation several times and was put on it, again, right before you got here. He had yelled at a young patient, causing her folks to request an emergency discharge.

"The high-ranked staff here at Maze have made an executive decision to terminate his employment. A replacement has been lined up and will start sessions this upcoming Monday. I urm," Oh no, he is losing his confidence, "was told to inform you. We are asking that all the interns be tolerant, and open-minded, during this time as it may cause the patients to struggle. They just need a brief period to adjust to the new therapist. Lacey will discuss that with you in-depth."

He may have been faltering in his well-pulled off business tone, but he was beginning to relax, which was comforting. The little crow's feet accenting his eyes begin to surface as he grins while talking. Michael is a truly kind guy. Clearly, this news could have not been more pleasing to either of us.

"You know June. I am honestly so relieved. I always had a strange feeling about the guy."
Michael pauses for a moment, staring down at his

slightly moist palms.

He hesitates before leaning over the desk, trying to get closer to me. He clumsily knocks a stapler off. In a hushed tone he says, "you probably do not know this, but my mother Glinda, she's actually a patient here."

I most certainly did not know that. How could such a conniving woman, that rarely stops blabbing, have raised such a sweet, soft-spoken son? I simply shake my head no.

"She can be a bit much, but she is my mom. I love her. I want her to be treated right. She is not well at all. To hear those complaints about Brooks, knowing that he is not only talking to but advising, my mother several times a week? It was awful." He inhales sharply while reeling back.

"I think Henry number three thought I was biased. Having your fresh perspective on him really made an impact. I'm really proud of you June, er, Miss Wilson." Michael assures me.

You know, I can see how the green tint to his hazel eyes mirrors the one in Glinda's. Though her smile often appears fake to me, it does favor Michael's genuine one, making me believe hers more. Seeing the kindness in Michael reminds me that I am not a psychologist. I have been too quick in judging Glinda. There has to be good there. I am just not being empathetic enough to seek it out. For that, I am almost as wrong as Dr. Brooks in making assumptions. I am so grateful that there are people like Michael to bring us all back to earth.

# CHAPTER FIFTEEN: RABID

It is not until the Tuesday after Michael speaks to me, that I realize I have roughly a week and a half of my Maze experience left. This is astonishing. Months in high school seemed to drag on for decades, but here? Two months at Maze feels like a three-day weekend. I have to be thankful and not get swamped with sadness though. That would be too narcissistic.

I finally feel like people genuinely enjoy me. I know guys like Evan exist. I know mean girls like Victoria can be avoided. I know learning to understand someone as complex as Randall can facilitate your own realizations and peace. I know life is real away from the people I have known for the past eighteen years. I am in awe. My last year of high school, I was truly starting to fear a sublime life.

That Tuesday morning, I set my tray down next to Evan's at breakfast. I stare at him for a minute.

"Hey, Evan? Do you think we could eat kinda quick, and then go grab some more coffee?"

"Of course, Juney-E," he agrees with his crooked smile. Asking Evan something is a formality. He is a go-with-the-flow guy, rarely having any objections.

After I pour a little more caramel creamer into my coffee than any adult should, I lead Evan out of the cafeteria. As we approach the sunroom, I can see Randall sitting on the closest rocker to us, alone. I plop down next to Randall. Evan eagerly sits on my other side.

Randall's face is priceless. He beams brightly at me and Evan. "Hi, June! Hi Evan! How are y'all this morning?" He inquires, his voice buzzing with excitement.

"We are wonderful, Randall! Is it okay if we join you for coffee?" I ask.

"I cannot think of anything I would enjoy more." He assures.

There we sit in peace, our eyes feasting on the deliciously green view. The full forest beyond the windows has increased in beauty and lush the longer I have been here. My gaze is instantly drawn to the spots where sunlight perfectly illuminates the trees. I can see the edge of the glittering creek embedded in earth. Randall's peculiar behavior in my peripheral vision suddenly reels in my attention. He is becoming fidgety, doing a strange trembling twitch with his fingers.

"You okay Randall?" I ask, concerned.

His hands instantaneously become still. I can see seriousness wash the color from his face before he speaks. "I had three visitors yesterday, June."

"Who?" I prompt. *This is not going to be pleasant.*

"One was Simon, my late bunkmate's wife. Her name is Julia. She visits me a good amount. She's a sweet girl, she was—" *Oh no.* I can see tears forming in his blue eyes.

Randall clears his throat and straightens his back before resuming. "Eight months pregnant when he died. They went at it like rabbits on his last leave. She had never brought the baby to see me. I never wanted her to, but yesterday, she did. Looking into her amber-colored eyes that matched his. That about killed me." Randall attempts a stabilizing breath, but all he can manage is a shallow flutter of air. *Today is racing downhill.*

"Randall, it's okay hun. That is sweet. She just wanted you to meet her." I attempt to console him, unsuccessfully.

"My ex came by later in the day. She has only visited me a couple of times. She started out fine, but then she began sobbing. Told me she could not help but be happy she ended it with me. All this time and I was still here. She said I would have ruined her life." Randall rests his head against his left palm as he finishes talking. I want this girl's address because it sounds like my fist needs to pay a visit to her face.

"You are so strong, Randall. Your day is going to come, man. You will get to go home so soon. I just know it." Evan interjects with little luck in persuading Randall.

"Thank you. I just feel like I was visited by the

ghosts yesterday. My ex the ghost of Christmas past because she no longer wants anything to do with me. Julia the ghost of Christmas present because she is still dealing with the tragedy I caused. Then, May, Simon's daughter, the ghost of Christmas future because she has no idea the sadness in store for her."

"Randall!" I exclaim. A sharp edge embedded in my tone. "You are kind. Don't ever compare yourself to Scrooge. You are a hero, Randall. You said you were close to a higher ranking. That's because you are valuable. You are brave. The government can stifle you, but please stop stifling yourself." Again, probably against the rules but Randall hugs me, motioning to Evan as well. We share a tight group hug.

"I need to go shower before my session with Dr. Mosh. You are sitting in, right June?" Randall inquires.

"Absolutely!" I promise.

"See you then." He says this while getting up and beginning to walk towards his room. Before he wanders out of ear-shot, he looks over his shoulder and says, "for the record. Y'all's words make me feel safe." *Bless his heart.*

Evan and I walk back to my room since we have a little over an hour to kill. Obviously, TV and talking is the best way to murder time. We discuss Randall and how desperately we wish we could help him. Alas, we have no clue how to execute such.

Evan can tell from my worried look how unsettled I am becoming. He attempts to shift the conversation to what he thinks to be a lighter topic.

"So, are you cool with me coming back with you at the end of next week and spending a couple of days with you, Juney-E?"

Ugh. I was dreading this question. This was a subject I had desperately been trying to avoid. "I don't know Evan, my family is…A little much." It was true. I mean Elizabeth lingered. He could not step foot in my house without seeing her pictures plastered to every square inch of drywall.

At first, Evan just seems to think I am embarrassed of my family. "I thought only one of your siblings was still at home though? So surely it can't be that crazy. If they are anything like you, I'll love them"

"My sister is all religious, and it creeps people out. You would be uncomfortable." I say, trying to maintain some logic.

"Well, maybe she can convert me then." Evan proposes his solution with an amused smile.

*Okay, ditch that bible-thumper, Delilah.* "My mom has one night stands a lot." I offer.

Evan is still not phased. "Hey, the more the merrier!"

He is morphing the situation into a joke. How can I argue with a joke? This is so damn hard. That grin weakens my knees.

"Evan, be serious." I hate to say it, but I cannot fabricate an alternative. My stomach begins to burn from stress-induced oversecretion.

Evan's smile falters a little, but he still makes one last attempt. "C'mon Juney! I just want to see where you grew up. It'll be fun!"

I cannot back down, not now. "I mean…"

"Are you like embarrassed of me or something?" Evan asks, an upset tone starting to invade his voice. How can I hurt him like this?

"What?! Evan no! I never would be. I just don't think you would enjoy being there. My cats... They can be very scratchy." *What the actual fuck, June.*

Yeah, Evan is officially done with the excuses. "You don't want me to come home with you because your cats...scratch? What's going on June?" He sounds so hurt, his voice chews on my will.

"Nothing. I just don't think it would be a good time. Me leaving for college soon and all." I reply, pleading for him to just accept this.

His tone shifts more towards anger than hurt as he states, "maybe you're not embarrassed."

*Finally, he is so right.* "Evan, I would never be. You are literally perfect." I assure him.

That is when he knocks me off my feet, not physically. *This is not a tale of domestic abuse.* He glares at me, his emerald eyes overrun with exasperation. "Maybe you just don't want me to meet your other boyfriend."

"Wait.... what...?" is all I can muster. I am so confused. *What is he implying.*

Evan instantly snaps back. "Yeah, I can see it. Girls can be so manipulative these days. It's hard to tell when they are just playing a part."

I still am not getting the big picture. "What in the world do you mean?"

In the harshest tone I can ever imagine Evan using, he says, "C'mon June, nobody is that shy. There always seems to be something a little fishy whenever I bring up your family, or friends, or anything to do with your hometown. You just want to pretend like you're a goody who chooses conversation over anything. The truth probably is that you don't want to have sex because you would feel too guilty. Maybe kissing and playing with my feelings is cool when you have a boyfriend back home, but sex, that would be too far now wouldn't it?"

I feel like a car, no a truck, a dang eighteen-wheeler, has just hit me then reversed over me, then hit me again. Yet somehow, I have to walk away from this. Heated saltwater streams down my hurt face. "I am going to be late to Randall's session. If you believe for a second that any of that's true. That I'm a lying whore. Then you're crazier than all of these patients combined."

# CHAPTER SIXTEEN: BESERK

On the way to Randall's session with Dr. Mosh, I have to duck into a communal bathroom and pull my disheveled self together. Trapped in a fog of harrowing bewilderment, a collapse conspired by secluded trauma has left me mistakenly wicked.

If I did not have a commitment, then I would have let my emotions detonate. I would have muffled sorrowful howls with a soaked pillow, but I don't live in a reality dominated by convenience. I need to look laminated with glossy professionalism. *Or just not like a hysterical catastrophe of runny makeup.* I use wads of quilted toilet tissue to wipe thick, goopy mascara from beneath my puffy eyes. A couple of deep breaths and a light slap on the face later, I emerge back into the hall.

Dr. Mosh's time with Randall seems to drone on for ages. I think I have developed legitimate wrinkles by now. Despite his upsetting talk with me a mere hour ago, Randall is now having a decent day. A quirky peace to his presence overthrows his usually anxious demeanor. Regardless of my gratuity for his lack of nervous ticking, I still find this session lacking in benefit.

Dr. Mosh's words are gratuitous. Makes his point and proceeds to elaborate on it to an irrelevant degree. I am starting to realize all of these alleged professionals display a façade of psychological wisdom. *Quacking ducks of doctors.* For Randall's sake, I try to conceal my disdain. It would be detrimental for him to misconstrue my disgust in this blatant malpractice as annoyance in his mental hardships. Finally, the session reaches a close, leaving me feeling drained to a point of minimal function.

My cozy bed beckons me, but because of this morning, I need to comfort Randall. I walk him back to his room like I do most days.

"Hey, June?" Randall asks, sheepishly, as we exit Dr. Quack's room.

"What's up?"

"Do you think we could take an extended route? Walk a few more halls than usual?" Randall requests. I agree as exercise releases brain-stabilizing endorphins.

Randall begins asking me a conglomerate of questions. "What are some of your favorite memories, June?"

"Uhhhh, probably my parents' divorce." I joke.

He laughs before further prompting. "Good one, but seriously, what do you think about when you are sad?"

I do not want to provide an actual answer to his question. All of my once-treasured memories inflame my heart with ache. I cannot keep Elizabeth out of the equation. "Well there was one time, my sisters, Lizzie and Delilah, my brother, Jamie, and I went to visit my oldest sister, Addison at college. She went to Coastal Alabama near Gulf Shores. Addison, and Jeff, the guy she would later marry, took us out to jet ski in the ocean. Which was, at first, terrifying.

"Delilah rode with Addison. They only made it a few yards out before Delilah started crying in fear. She was convinced the jet-ski was bound to spontaneously combust." Randall giggles as I continue.

"Everybody wanted me to ride by myself, but I was way too intimidated. The waves were monstrous. So, Lizzie let me ride with her. She went insane, she would do donuts one way, then immediately reverse to do them the opposite way, creating rifts strong enough to topple the machine right on over. Which she did, twice." I have to pause and chuckle.

"Could not have phased her less. The girl was wild. After the second time, she had to coax me into crawling back on. Then, she took off, me barely even having a grasp on her life vest. She went full speed, creating a high bounce when the jet-ski met the rocky waves. The seat made a wish-bone out of my legs, and I was too sore to walk the next day. I don't know, it was still probably the most fun times I have ever had. I really wish I had been brave enough to drive my own." I sniffle, starting to tear up as the flashes of salty breeze and wind-blown skin replay in my mind.

"I love that, June," Randall says. I think he can sense the melancholy undertone drifting through my cheerful story. "Who is your biggest hero?"

"Charles Manson cause he does his own thing." again, Randall snickers, but I can tell he wants a real answer.

"Probably Zelda Fitzgerald. I love F. Scott, but so much of his work was inspired by her. She lived it, and he wrote it. I find beauty in her allowing him to share her struggle. She was so sick, her mind so compromised with illness, yet she still had a light that ignited the world's most exquisitely breathtaking literature." I reply, feeling a release in embracing authenticity.

"Wow, so, I guess asking your favorite book would be a waste of time?" Randall asks, a light-hearted shimmer sparkling in his eyes.

"Well, the answer is not Gatsby," I admit. "Short story may be a better place to start. 'Winter Dreams' is another of Fitzgerald's pieces. It's about a man in love with ideas. He calls his desire for romance and material success his winter dreams, but when they find him, he turns to mourn their loss. The cold realities of petty hearts and shallow fame make him aware that he only adores his imagined reality. The one he has been fabricating since youth. The one that will never fully exist."

"I would love to read that June, it sounds… enchantingly raw." Randall comments.

"It is," I assure. "Gatsby, however, I read in sophomore year English class. I was mesmerized by the eloquent writing and paralleled pain. Then, the girl sitting behind me asked why Daisy was crying over shirts. I told her they symbolized all the years she had lost with the love of her life. That the grief of what could have been was finally overwhelming her. The girl informed me that I was weird. That they were just shirts. So, after that, the book left a bitter taste of disappointment in my mouth. It was the moment I officially lost all faith in my peers."

"People are ignorant, June. The smaller their world, the tighter their range of emotion, the easier." Randall responds. At this point, we are back to his room. I follow him in.

He perches himself on the edge of his bed. His eyes, now quizzical, look over to me. His stare burns. I begin to squirm uncomfortably under his purposeful gaze. Finally, he slices the silence, his tone timid. "What's your biggest regret June?"

I take in the view of scuffed floor for a moment before answering. I consider lying, but what was the point? Randall is an honest guy. He did not deserve to have his questions deflected.

I sit in the wooden chair across from his bed. "I don't think I love my sister enough."

"She passed away, didn't she June? The girl driving your jet-ski?" I have wanted to tell Randall about Elizabeth for weeks. I simply had not been courageous enough to do so. Though I knew he would understand, plaguing him with my gloom seemed like too much of a burden. I did, at one point, mention something bad had happened to one of my sisters. I felt like for all he knew, it could have been a simple broken arm. I was wrong; his instincts too sharp.

Randall can tell from the sweat now beading on my brow, and the chatter in my teeth, that I am stumped in cultivating a response. "When somebody is processing death, their mind is altered. Your thinking pattern shifts. After a few conversations with you, I could tell that from the way in which you thought, that you had suffered a loss. I noticed because it is how I think too. I am still locked in grief for the men I could not save. You also seem to be entrapped by tragedy." I am unnerved by his statement.

"What do you mean?" I ask, my voice increasing in pitch. "I am not grieving anymore. She has been dead for four years. I don't care anymore."

"June, she was your sister. It is okay to care. In fact, you should care," assures Randall. His tone is now drenched in concern.

I feel my hand quiver as it rests on my thigh. "No, you don't understand. I still care about her. I do love her. It's just, she ruined everything. I don't care that she is dead anymore. I am over it." My eyes beg him to leave the subject in safe solitude.

"What happened to her June?" Randall inquires.

"Randall, I don't talk about it." I insist. Though I am developing a subtle want to let the suppressed story out.

"I did not want to talk about my incident either, but eventually I was forced to. You know what? It helps, a lot, tell me. Just take your time. It'll be okay." Randall is maintaining the eye contact I keep trying to break. I feel like his gaze will hypnotize me into verbal expulsion.

I resist the urge to ask if telling the story will bring her back because that is the only way this could be okay. I take a substantial breath before diving into the story that wrecked me.

"When I was a freshman in high school, I took a drama class. I had to do a personal monologue. Elizabeth's death was fresh so, though I hate to admit it, I did a speech on her passing. Since then, I have had those words memorized, ingrained in my mind. So, if this sounds rehearsed that's why." I inform Randall. He nods encouragingly. I swat my finger as my nail instinctively digs into my cheek.

"I awoke to screams. Blood-curdling, skin peeling, tooth pulling screams. The screams of my mother, my father, and my oldest sister. All I could do was shake; convulse in dread for what would proceed. I knew I should not be scared for my own life. The screams that were turning into winded chokes, were not of imminent danger or physical pain. They were of insanity. I could not cry. My thinking was barricaded from reason. My mind thickened with heavyset murk.

"I was startled when I felt my sister, Delilah, wrap her trembling body around mine. She said nothing because she had nothing to say. We possessed the same amount of knowledge. All we were aware of was that the life we knew had disintegrated.

"Eventually, my oldest sister, Addison, stumbled through my doorway. She did not so much as hover her hand over the light switch. She simply hobbled to my bed and crawled in. The words, 'there's been an accident and Lizzie is not coming home' sounded from her shaky mouth.

I pause to steady my own lips. "I am sorry, but I cannot describe how hearing that made me feel. I don't have the will to risk re-feeling that way."

"It is okay, June. It was painful, I know. Just tell me what happened next." Randall interjects.

"I laid there sobbing, but instead of holding on to Delilah I slid away. I crept to the edge of my bed and curled myself into a tight ball. She barely noticed my movement and simply slid into Addison's sturdy arms. I remember the grief overwhelming Addison. Swallowing her whole. She later told me that her thoughts were gone, and all she could do was feel. Feeling is so dangerous.

"A couple of hours later somebody, I'm still not sure who, got a hold of Jamie. He practically flew from the apartment he had been sharing with his ex-fiancée. That relationship did not last through Elizabeth's death. He was wounded too deeply, and she could not fix him fast enough. His pain was just not equivalent to hers. How could it be? She may have loved Elizabeth, but she was our sister, not hers. Naturally, she wanted to move on to brighter days, and he was still held back. So, she told him that perhaps they would be together in another lifetime. Jamie replied by ordering her to get the fuck out of his sight. That was that." I stop again, not wanting to go back to describing the actual event.

"Crazy how death can kill more than just a person," Randall adds. I nod before resuming.

"When Jamie got to our house that night, he too

laid in my bed. There we were. All the Wilson kids writhing in sorrow. Or should I say all the Wilson kids left. We were in that bed for the remainder of the night. Honestly, we were cramped on that queen-sized mattress the majority of the next day as well." *A girl in my drama class, sporting braces and a severe underbite, had called me inbred for admitting that.*

I remember easing in and out of tears, sleep, and clarity. I recall my siblings arguing with themselves. Attempting to make peace. I knew peace was not possible, not yet."

I chuckle softly before continuing. "This may sound bizarre, but I just kept thinking of the short story, 'The Monkey's Paw.' It's the one about a magical paw that allows you to make three wishes. It falls into a family's hands, and they decide to use the paw, even though, they have been warned that every wish has a consequence. The family starts by wishing for a large sum of money. The next morning, they are disappointed to find no trace of the cash. Later in the day, the mother and father are informed that their son has been killed at his employing factory. The pension they will receive is the exact amount they had originally wished for.

"The mother then uses the paw to will her child back to life. The father knows that there will again be severe costs. That, if he returns, his son will be in sinister condition. He pries the paw from his delirious wife and wishes his son back to death. The end of the story used to confuse me. I could never understand why the father's third wish came true without consequence. That is when I understood that wishing his baby dead was the consequence.

"The parents would not be tortured further because that was enough. I found comfort in this story because I thought maybe this was it. Maybe my family would be spared of pain for a while. I guess that was my shred of peace. Really, I just wanted my fucking sister to come home no matter how insidious she may be.

"Around 8 o'clock, on the day following Elizabeth's death, my Aunt Rachel, my Aunt Millie, and my Uncle Franklin tiptoed into my room. My Aunt Rachel announced that it was time to get ready to go to the funeral home. Just like that, we were supposed to be okay enough. None of us were expected to be fully functioning; we just had to be decent enough to be in public. I know no one would have judged us if we had not been, but I also knew we needed to be.

"Plus, I wanted a break from the silent agony. My aunts helped push us girls in and out of the shower, one by one. At points, I could not tell if I was crying or if the lukewarm water was just splashing my face. After that, they blew dry and curled each of our heads of thick hair. Then a multi-toned maroon and brown dress was forced over my body.

"Around 9:30, I descended down my home's wide-curved stairs. At their base, I saw my parents for the first time. Obviously not for the first time in my life, but the first time since Elizabeth had passed away. I could not bear to look at them. Their expressions were hopeless. I did not know how to react or process; I felt like my insides were rotting. I slid behind Addison in hopes that she could shield me from their stare; the attempt failed.

"My mother ran and clung to us. I was thankful when my Aunt Rachel pulled her off and informed her of the time. My mom nodded and she, my father, Rachel, and Franklin departed in Rachel's SUV. My siblings and I rode with my estranged Aunt Millie to the funeral home.

"Bergman's is a decent parlor. The staff is nice. The venue is clean. A surplus of family, friends, and food greeted us there. It is slightly comical how people think food will mend anything. Throw a veggie platter, an array of deli meats, and a gallon of sweet tea together, and you have got yourself a solution. I wish it worked like that. I know people do what they can. Nobody has the ability to fix the real problem, so they try to soften it.

"The whole day was filled with condolences and waterworks. People I barely knew were kissing me on the cheek, combing their fingers through my hair, and trying to tell me it was for the best. That Elizabeth was in a better place now. That was the worst. It was almost impossible to nod and agree. But I knew an explosion of argument would be detrimental. I knew I had to hold in my opinions. Elizabeth believed in God, and I was going to respect my sister.

"Elizabeth's best friend showed up around noon. Her name is Anna, but she goes by a combination of her first and middle name, so its Anna Grace. She will straight up ignore you if you forget. Anna, along with their friend Layla, found Elizabeth."

"June?" Randall murmurs. "What happened to her? I know it's easier to talk about the aftermath, but I think you need to say how she died."

I shift my mouth to the side and look up at the ceiling's lazily spinning fan. I want to resist letting the building tears overflow. "I don't….." I whisper.

"She was just so fucking stupid, Randall," I admit, and hold the bridge of my nose in an attempt to calm myself. I barely muster the strength to continue.

"In the proximity of Eufaula lies Walter F. George Lake. Lizzie and eight of her friends were there celebrating graduation. They were drinking. I mean it was their first night of freedom. My parents allowed Elizabeth to attend this get together. They knew alcohol would be present, but they trusted her to not be an idiot.

"Elizabeth had a boyfriend named Greg. They dated pretty much the majority of high school. According to their friends, Greg and Elizabeth had gotten into an intense argument soon after arriving at the lake. They wandered into the surrounding wilderness to maintain the privacy of their squabble.

"When confronted by police, Greg said that they were arguing about the future. He was backing out of UA, wanted to go with his safety school instead. That was not Lizzie's plan, and she wanted them to be together. After the climax of their altercation, Greg stormed off. He claims he left Elizabeth weeping on a mossy tree stump. He insists that she was merely a short walk from their campsite. Elizabeth knew precisely how to get back, I am sure she did, but her emotions overrode her sane reasonings. She stumbled further into the woods in a drunken haze. I assume she had no motivation other than the fact that the farther she got from her antagonizer, the better she felt.

"Once Greg returned, he told the others the main gist of what had happened. I am sure he said some ugly things about her. What does it matter? That's his burden to bear. Anna and Layla scolded Greg and ran off to comfort their best friend.

"Unfortunately, it was too late. The entirely trashed girls stumbled upon my sister's corpse, lying a good twenty feet beneath them. Lizzie was floating, face-down, in the clouded lake water. She had been, of course, hurt, and frustrated. She was not paying an ounce of attention as to where she was walking. Presumably, Elizabeth unknowingly gravitated towards the lake's border, overstepped on the path, and tumbled down a drop-off. Her head collided with a rock, fracturing her skull, and knocking her unconscious. She drowned in a little over a foot of water.

"Anna had her cell on her, and surprisingly, had service. She immediately dialed 911 as they rushed down to Elizabeth. By the time the girls got to her, she was gone. Though they tried to revive her, it became painstakingly obvious that her eyes would never blink again.

Anna continued to attempt CPR until the medics arrived because she had watched enough Grey's to know it was worth the effort. The rest of the party had not gone looking for them until the paramedics arrived. Of course, this sent everyone into a confused frenzy.

"Eventually, they found the girls. Elizabeth was pronounced dead on the scene. Her time of death 10:07 PM. The night was still early. Her life was still early." I guess it did feel a little relieving to verbally uncork that nightmare of a memory for the first time.

"Back to the funeral, Anna stepped inside and was suddenly the focus. What can I say? My town was, is, obsessed with high school popularity. Even Anna noticed the immediate shift. She strode over to me and Jamie, who I was sitting with at the time, and apologized. I asked her what for. She said, 'more than everything.' I remember shuddering because it felt like a movie line. The only problem is that a dramatic and meaningful song did not play as a tear-overwhelmed Anna stormed back through Bergman's doors. I still hope she was being genuine and not trying to garner sympathy.

"The next day was a replay of the previous one. Viewings are just a form of preparation. In both the concrete and abstract sense. The entire time I was just bracing myself for the actual funeral. The sealing of the deal.

"On the third day since Elizabeth's death, I woke up-weighted. I knew this day was going to be one of the most difficult days I had ever, may ever, experience. I was tempted to just stay in bed and let the sadness engulf me.

"Alas, I got up. Maybe for Elizabeth, maybe for the rest of my family, maybe for myself. I don't know. Rachel was the one who had woken me. Her and Millie started to perform the same routine they had executed the past two days. Except this time, the process was elevated. Instead of leaving my hair down, they twisted it up into an elegant chignon. They slathered the usual foundation and such on me but added blush, champagne-colored eyeshadow, waterproof mascara, and finishing the look off with rose-colored lipstick.

"Last night, my aunts had bought all of us new clothes for the occasion. I slipped the heavy iridescent earrings, they had purchased, into my empty piercings. Then I stepped into my new, midnight-black gown. I turned and took a look into the full-length mirror on the back of mine and Delilah's bathroom door. The dress was high-necked and sleeveless. It was fitted until right below the waist where the crinoline layer caused the gown to flow out until the chiffon material reached its end right above my knee cap. If it had been light pink, it would have been perfect for a ballerina.

"I looked gorgeous. How could I look my best on that day? Then I realized something, I was now the prettiest girl in the family. Elizabeth and Jamie had always been the best looking. Now it was me and him. I felt guilt wash through me. I still feel guilty for thinking that. I smacked my reflection and wiped off the lipstick in shame."

"Sometimes we just can't control what comes through our minds, June. After all, thoughts are just that…. thoughts. nothing more, nothing less." Randall interjects. I appreciate his kindness, but I still resent that fleeting moment.

"We walked into Eufaula First Baptist Church. I had never been inside it before. We were not really churchgoers. I almost laughed when I realized that was where her service would be held. Lizzie was a southern belle. Though she never attended church services, she would refer to Jesus Christ as her savior on occasion. I guess I should not have been surprised that her funeral would be held there.

"Elizabeth only talked about her faith in front of others. She was like that. Lizzie wanted everyone to hold a certain image of her. She put an unimaginable amount of pressure on herself to be perfect. Honestly, I have no idea what Lizzie actually believed. Looking back, I don't know that much about the real Elizabeth. I don't think she knew that much about herself yet." My voice is becoming strained, and my vocals dry. *I need water.*

"I understand that. It is easy to get caught up in the lies you tell not only to others but to your mind." Randall comments as he reads my mind and grabs a mini-bottle of spring water from the mini-fridge under his dorm-like bed. "Maybe they are not lies if you believe them too."

"They just certainly are not the truth," I reply before chugging half the bottle in one gulp.

"The whole procession aspect was simultaneously embarrassing and gut-wrenching. I am shocked I did not puke. I always imagined that I would walk down the aisle before Lizzie, me wearing an unflattering bridesmaid dress, her clothed in a white taffeta gown, glowing like an angel. Now I was following her, except she was hidden in plain sight, entrapped within a closed box. I guess that way, she really was an angel. Anyway, I recall everyone in attendance turning to visually preen my family and I as we took tiny baby-steps down the stained carpet. I could feel a mixture of judgment and pity radiating from their glazed eyes. All I could do was look down and weep inaudibly.

"The moment we were seated, the preacher began his sermon. He acted as if he had somewhere better to be. His main focus was to save 'lost' souls, not to honor Elizabeth's life. Oh, and to talk about himself and condescend others. He adored that. I remember my body brimming with hate and disgust. The prick ruined Lizzie's last event. She was not going to graduate from college. She was not going to be thrown a bachelorette party, or a baby shower. That was it; that was all Elizabeth got.

"I should have intervened. I should have been brave and stood up and told the morosely obese man to stop. He probably would have backed down like a wounded puppy. I would have dented his pride so thoroughly. How could I? It would have destroyed my mom and Addison. The most persuading factor, though, was knowing how much my interruption would have mortified Lizzie.

"When the fraud was finally finished sputtering spite, Layla, one of the friends that found her spoke, followed by an elderly family friend. The smug preacher then got up and concluded the mess with a prayer. I could not even muster the energy to give a damn.

"It was sinking further into my consciousness that this was it. Nail in the coffin so to speak. So, too literally speak. It was now the part where we all had to walk around the casket and see Elizabeth before she was buried. I remember looking down at my sister and feeling taunted.

"People say that after someone's dead, their body only looks like a vacant shell. A shadow of the person who used to dwell within, I disagree, they look asleep. I wanted to shake the daylights out of my sister. Make her come back. It was impossible to believe that she really could not. That she was not just playing opossum. It was Lizzie, it was my sister. We had watched *A Cinderella Story* together just five nights ago. She looked exactly the same." My stored tears have abandoned all hope in staying in their ducts. They spill out, blurring my view of Randall, starting to make me feel more detached from the room as a whole.

"Seeing her was without a doubt the hardest part. The burial turned out to be the easiest. I was so incredibly relieved to be over with the whole situation. Even comforted, for the circus of an event to be at its close. I was desperate to start healing.

"And like." *My voice is thickening like a sauce that has just been doused with flour.* "I know she was destined for greatness, but sometimes we can't be who we were meant to be. I guess it's up to luck to see if we get to live out our lives, or if we only get to be memories in somebody else's."

"I completely understand, June." Randall agrees. "Was that kind of the end of the drama? I mean did you finally get some time to regroup, maybe go to therapy?"

"Kind of. well, there was this thing with Greg, Lizzie's boyfriend. Like two weeks after the funeral, I was on my couch, napping with my cat, when I heard a timid knock at the front door.

"At the time, I was not the least bit startled.

People I barely knew had been stopping by constantly to drop off lasagnas or fruit baskets. I recall thinking that if I put one more forkful of overcooked noodles in my mouth I was going to engage in a homicidal rampage.

"I groggily answered the door, sloppily sporting rat-nest hair and smudged glasses. I was a bit caught off guard to see Greg's sunken face opposite mine. My initial reaction was to tell him that Elizabeth was not home. Though the ironic truth, that was obviously no longer an option. I remember feeling an internal shudder surge through me as I realized that.

"I actually did not speak. I waited. Greg broke like a doomed promise. I recall feeling my face twitching in discomfort as I watched him burst into inconsolable hysterics. Honestly, I did not want his sorrowful meltdown in my life. It was not appropriate for Greg to just come over to his deceased girlfriend's home and fall apart in front of her traumatized sister.

"Nevertheless, I beckoned him in. He sulked inside and plopped down on the couch. I sat on the farthest cushion from him. I remember being puzzled. Did he want to see my whole family? My parents? Jamie? Addison? Then he started murmuring sorry over and over and over again. I just nodded. I was not going to comfort him. Why should I? I'm the victim here. My family is the victim. He abandoned her there, drunk, and senseless.

"That is when I noticed that his skin was turning a pale shade of green, like seafoam. I was suddenly covered in his sick. I called for my mom right as he yanked a prescription pill bottle from his back pocket and threw it to the ground. It was so damn dramatic.

"He had made her death about him. My mom rushed down the stairs and got him to the ER in time to pump his stomach. After that, my family forgave him. They probably never even blamed him. I don't hold it against him either. I am not saying it was all Greg's fault. Lizzie was responsible as well. I have enough sense to let it go and forgive."

As I am concluding Elizabeth's story, I am smacked with the harsh reality. It is over. I had started telling the story slowly as if I was hoping someone would jump in and stop me. Sometimes when I rewatch an upsetting movie or reread a tragic story, I feel a certain anxiety mixed with hope. I am subconsciously willing for the plot to end differently this time.

I try to trick my mind into thinking things will work out this time.

Maybe the central conflict won't arise. Of course, it inevitably does, and I feel the standard rush of sadness. I am not naive or stupid. I just want it to work out so desperately that I almost trick myself into thinking I can will an alternate ending. Crazy, I know, but that's how I felt talking about Elizabeth's death. I wanted to say that a miracle happened. That she was revived, or that they found her as she was about to slip, and for a millisecond, I almost believe the fantasy.

Of course, that is the finale. Her story has been

told. That's where it ends.

Towards the end of my explanation, Randall looks at me with eyes that swim in a mixture of deep concern, a distinct unease, and even a hint of fear. I know he is biting his tongue. He is obviously mentally weighing the pros and cons of whatever he is hesitating to say.

I get it, I had just unloaded heaps of information on him. Probably, had upset him with the bleakness of the ordeal. I have a feeling, though, that I might not like what he is about to say. After a minute of watching him process his thoughts, I relent. "Just tell me, Randall. It's okay." *I should not have chosen sorry over safe.*

"I think you are lying." Randall breaks from my gaze the moment he leaks such an accusation.

"Go on." I encourage calmly, inside feeling like a mangled mess of nerves.

"People say forgive and forget as if it is the easiest thing in the world. Forgetting is impossible. Unless you have a traumatic brain injury, or you have rocks in your head, then you simply cannot let parts of your life fade from memory. It is a completely unrealistic concept. Forgiveness is possible though, June." Randall says, still not elaborating on why he thinks I am shielding him from the truth.

"The thing is, I don't think you had enough sense to not hold everything against your sister and her boyfriend. I think that sense is a facade. I'm starting to believe you have a horribly weighted grudge against your sister, her boyfriend, and everyone else involved. I also think you are scared to validate Greg hurting himself because it makes it all so much more tragic. I believe this grudge and fear haunts you every hour of every day

"I don't think you can let the situation be. I think you pick at it and continue to let that wound fester. Please don't take offense because I desperately want this to help you. I also think you are wrong about it being a matter of sense. It does not make you more or less sensible to feel this way.

"It's separate. This is an emotional problem that has sunk so deep, that sense has been overridden and to no fault of your own. Well, to no conscious fault of your own. June, if you do not start to genuinely forgive and lift some of that dense pain, then I don't know if sense will ever be back in the equation. I do not believe you will be able to understand and completely process your sister's death without that sense. You are by far the most level-headed person I have ever had the pleasure to meet. I know you have strong ideals and realistic reasonings. You just need to let that wipe out some of this debilitating emotion. The only way to do that is to truly start to forgive." Wow, I have just been shrinked by a patient. *A good one at that.*

I try to explain myself. "In my case, the inability to forget makes me unable to forgive. In order to forgive Greg, I would have to analyze him, their relationship, his role in her death. It's not worth it. Stupid Greg is not worth all of that. He can handle my resentment better than I can handle my thoughts."

I feel Randall's almond-shaped eyes burn into me. He knows I am stumbling in my mind, fighting myself. I am aware that I am barely making sense. I am not even really responding to what he has said. I am transitioning to illogical rambling.

"If I have to attempt to forgive him, I'll subconsciously begin trying to forgive Elizabeth. That's the bottom line: I do not want to forgive my sister. You are right. I have harbored the nastiest, gravitationally-strong grudge against her since the moment she was lowered into the ground. It's more than a grudge, I think... I believe... I can't even say it." I pause, pierce my delicate lip tissue with my sharp teeth.

"I hate her. I hate Elizabeth. I hate my sister. I know I have good memories, great memories with her. I try and try to remember that, but my heart swells with hatred every time I hear her damn name. I think *that bitch. That selfish bitch.* She ruined my family. It was not that great to begin with, so now the dynamic is virtually nonexistent.

"My siblings, my parents feel like obligations. I know they feel it too. Like we are forced by nature to interact. The love other families feel is stale and dry in mine. The love is still there, but it is sour like forgotten milk. She yanked all the light from our world and then blinded us from seeing any more.

"All I want to talk about is her, all I think about is her. Everything leads back to her. Sometimes, I wish I could take that pill that rape victims take to forget. I feel like I have to erase her existence in order to have a life. Who thinks like that? Who wants to forget somebody that they adore? How can anyone hate what they love? How do those emotions co-exist? How the fuck will I ever get past this?" My body is trembling to the point of making the chair shake.

Randall gapes at me. His eyes sadden to an almost inhuman point. I am crumbling. The words were spilling from my mouth faster than I could process them. With every word, a piece of me had shattered like a smashed mirror. With every word, I wondered more if this was it, was this my breaking point. The point of no return. I can feel crippling terror creep up my dehydrated throat. Horrified by what I have just confessed, I bolt. I cannot stand to be in that room a moment longer. Hell, I cannot stand to be in my skin a moment longer.

I need to hug Evan. Indifference is all I feel towards our earlier fight. I want him to hold me so tight that air can only escape my lungs in meager pants. I need him to murmur comforts in my ear, assure me that crying is okay. I sprint in the direction of his room, expecting to swipe the skeleton key and wander in. To my dismay he is not snuggled up in his bed, sobbing whilst listening to Whitney Houston, as I imagined he might be after our argument.

Instead, he is in the hall with Victoria. Whispers fleeing to his ear from her satisfied lips. Her hand gently rubs his back in small circles. I freeze, cold air escaping my chest in a subtle gasp. A few moments go by before they notice me standing there, tears flowing like a rampant river down my face, now soaking my scrubs.

When Evan's weary eyes meet mine, a look of panic spreads across his face. He lunges to approach me as I back away. "June, are you okay hun?

Victoria was just telling me—"

I cut him off as my voice escalates to a hysterical yell. "My sister is fucking dead Evan! I do not have another boyfriend at home. I have a dead sister that I can't talk about. Okay?!"

His stride towards me had halted the moment I began speaking. Once I finish, he resumes, pleading, "Juneyyyyy."

I trip over the hastiness of my backward shuffle, causing me to stumble as I point my finger at him in warning. "No! No, Evan. Do not get near me. You mentioned sex earlier. Well, guess what? I am sure Victoria's unshaven legs are wide open."

Movement sounding from one of the surrounding rooms startles me. Perhaps roaring my thunderous disdain was not such a bright idea. Literally, have never heard my voice ascend to such a booming volume. *I am in so much trouble.* I gallop to the stairs, my feet procuring leaps and bounds, deserting Evan as he looks at me in mystified disbelief, his feet cemented to the thin carpet.

# CHAPTER SEVENTEEN: CRACKED

The only place I can fathom being empty at this point in the day is the only place I am forbidden from. *The shock therapy room.* The rules are now obsolete. They always were. I arrive at my hiding place just in time for my exhausted lungs to start the process of choking suffocation. I slide down the wall and onto the cold, depressing tile.

As I feel the uncontrollable sobs rock my body, I embrace the unconventional comfort. I know how to cry. Hell, I am good at it. I know, though it is a feeling of utter desolation, that it cannot actually hurt me. Weeping is simply a harmless, meaningless reaction. The cause is the real issue. The actual pain. Facing the confession that has inflicted such unsettlement, that is brimming with devastating potential. Crying is not. It is just hot, salty liquid. There is no danger in sitting here and allowing that water to run like a damn faucet.

The distinct sound of sneakers squeaking against floor adds to my wailing. I lift my heavy-as-a-sack-of-flour head up. At first, worried that I have been caught by an orderly. To my astonishment, I see Evan, his face uncharacteristically solemn.

Here I am, wallowing on the ground, both knees bent up to my chin. I feel my face crumble like a piece of soon-to-be-discarded tin foil before I return my head to resting in my slick palms. I am incapable of gathering enough strength to acknowledge Evan. The sobs course through my body harder than before. *So much fucking harder*. I could easily burst a blood vessel from the intensity.

Once Evan processes what in God's name I am doing, he swiftly shuts and deadbolts the door. *Guess Maze truly wants to be thorough when trapping patients in here*. Evan slides his back down the wall to sit beside me. At first, I feel a surge of fearful anticipation when considering what Evan might say. That fear is short-lived. Though I am the epitome of delicate, I have already hit rock bottom. Evan can do no further damage.

He gently pulls me across his lap. Evan places me in the position people hold their newly betrothed in as they cross the threshold of their new home. Initially, I resist his warmth, still fuming with anger at him. I surrender soon enough, mentally holding up a white flag. I defeatedly bury my face in the hollow of his shoulder.

Evan lets me cry out my emotions fully, without any attempt at intervention. He knows I need to be soothed. His gentle hands caress my back in soft intervals. He rests his cheek on top of my messy hair. Though I am unhappy with him, I am so grateful for his comforting embrace. If Evan had not chased after me, I am sure I would have panicked to the point of vomiting. *Lord knows I did not need to do that.*

"I am really sorry about your sister. I'm sure that must have been earth-shattering." The emphatic result of my slaughtered secret. At least he is not upset with me for lying.

Evan makes my heart pounce when he roughly grips either side of my shoulders, his eyebrows knit with genuine concern as he stares directly into my overflowing eyes. His tone is firm as he says, "June, that's what Victoria was telling me. She caught me sitting alone at lunch and started plaguing me with questions about why I looked so sulky. I told her we had fought. I didn't want to tell her anything else, but you know how she is. She kept pressing. I ended up telling her details as we left the cafeteria. I'm sorry. I was just totally disgruntled. It felt good to vent.

"When I said the other boyfriend part, she started snickering. She's honestly a dreadful person. I hope she gets gonorrhea. Anyways, at that point, we were close to my room. She looked around and told me to come close. Victoria whispered in my ear, 'she's trying to keep you from knowing she has a dead sister, moron. She lies about it to everyone.' I was processing the information when you walked up. That was also when I realized she had her hand on my back. I have no clue when she put it there, probably saw you first and did it out of spite." I study his pupils carefully, waiting for them to dart.

However, his gaze remains unbroken as he continues. "I had just found out my girl was in pain, and the gravity of what I had said to you hit me. *Hard.* I was not paying an ounce of attention to her. Victoria could have slapped me, and I would have barely noticed."

Evan pulls my body closer, still making sure our eyes stay locked. Tremors begin to invade his voice. "June I am so unimaginably sorry for what I said. I love you Juney-E. I really, really do." His rich green eyes begin to well.

So much is co-occurring. Where do I even begin? The fact that Evan now knows my tragic fib? The fact that Victoria should be lynched? The fact that Evan loves me, and I am 95% sure I love him back? Meanwhile, I am still trapped in a haze of guilt over admitting to hating my sister for having a life that ended prematurely.

As I am attempting to absorb this storm of information, Evan resumes talking. He sounds tentative, maybe even a bit fearful. The tears that had been welling in his eyes are now streaking down his face. "I have not been that truthful about my own family. I'm not an only child. Well, I don't know. Ugh, I hate saying that. I hate lying about it. It's just...too intense." His voice is riddled with cracks and quivers.

At first, I am itching with unsettlement. Typically, when people cry in front of me, I become… *inappropriate.* I feel extremely awkward and lose a vital sense of control. This usually results in unsolicited giggles. This time, however, I feel oddly okay.

"When you grow up with free-spirited and mother-nature loving parents, you feel masked from the mainstream world. You do not consider yourselves quite as vulnerable to society's problems, or at least I know I didn't. My mom and dad had some fertility problems, but, when I was ten, she finally got pregnant. It was quite the shock. A great one though.

"My parents were overjoyed, and I was so excited to be a big brother. When my parents went to their three-month ultrasound, there were some uh... complications. They did not know how severe it would be, but the outlook was far from good.

"My brother was diagnosed with a rare disease called osteogenesis imperfecta, a mouthful. It basically means that he had little to no chance of sustaining life. He would most likely die within a few hours of birth. His bones were brittle and splintering, even within the womb. Like I said, my parents are pretty earthy. Though the time frame made it an option, they decided against termination.

My folks hoped and prayed that somehow the world would provide and, if carried to term, the baby could be born normally. They wanted the ultrasound to be incorrect so badly that they tricked themselves into believing that they would receive, well, a miracle. As you can probably guess, they did not." Evan grits his teeth in anguish after spitting those last three words.

"Took me three years to learn how to pronounce his disease. Only took it three hours to kill him. My mama was in natural labor for two whole days. I think, in a way, she wanted to hold on. The second he was out, the closer he was to leaving us.

"My parents had me come and stay in the room about a half hour after he was born. I got to hold him. At that point, they were not even trying to make him live on a machine. The love amazed me, but so did the pain. It just was not fair. He was a baby. A helpless, little baby. I stayed until he died in my mother's arms.

"I watched the doctors pry him away as she shook uncontrollably. My dad wanted to comfort her, but he was in a trance. He dragged a wet washcloth across her sweaty forehead, but his eyes were vacant. I crawled into bed with my mom and hugged her as she embraced the unbearable hurt. I tried to tell her it was okay. I was her baby. I was here. But I think her agony, her grief, had blocked her hearing. She was submerged in devastation. It was so surreal, and again unfair."

Hearing his story feels like a thousand needles are pricking my mind and body. I try to offer some condolences by saying, "Evan I'm so—" but he cuts me off.

Evan is clearly still consumed in his story, not wanting to pause because then he would lose the will to continue. I completely understand. You must verbalize haunting memories rapidly before they fall back into the painful pits of silence within your soul, where you stifled them before.

"I never got to be a big brother. I never got to throw the football around or talk to him about girls. I wanted to teach him to ski, and swim, and so much more." At this point Evan is practically bawling, words wheezing from his throat between dense breaths. "I know having memories can make dealing with a death so much worse, but never getting that opportunity, never knowing a person you love so much, only seeing them live a God-awful life, that is almost smothering."

My squabbling mirrors my boyfriend's as I feel the insatiable want to take away his aching pain. "Evan? Maybe we should move to the bed." I suggest, wanting to hold each other tight enough to squeeze out the suffering. *Yes, by bed I meant shock therapy treatment cot.*

Evan agrees. We lay there for a solid half hour, indulging in hugs and sobs, not even trying to console each other vocally. Once we have both settled down, I feel the need to ask him a question. A question that could easily cause the waterworks to return. I must ask though. The remorse I feel about my perceptions of Elizabeth is still burning into my soul, branding me with indignity.

"Evan?" I murmur with what little breath I have not exhausted. He supplies me with an encouraging look. "Do you.." Oh no my voice is faltering. *Pull it together, girl.*

"Do you ever wonder how it would have been if your brother had never been conceived? If you had strictly been an only child? Would it be better to be scarred, or to have never known the wonderful person who cut you?" I do not even glance at him as I talk. I am astounded to even be saying these words aloud.

"I loved, love, my sister so much. Sometimes, I wonder how it would have been if she was never my sister. If I didn't go through that trauma. I know it would be giving up, and taking back, so much. I just feel like maybe the intense pain from the loss of such a close relationship is more prominent than the joy of it?"

Evan does not answer immediately. I feel shame trickle into my system. "I am awful. I am an awful person. I just think these things, and they gnaw at me. I feel crazy, and I panic, and I'm sorry." My slur executes to be redundant and ridiculous. I have excised my tear reservoir, so I begin dry crying. *Like a fucking hound dog.*

Spans of silence lug on before Evan responds. "I think that depth is a scary thing, and when grief is mixed with it you can't tell up from down or left from right. The truth is, I have considered which one would be better almost every day since he died. At various points in my life, I have different opinions about it.

"When I was twelve, I even yelled at my mom, saying that I wish they had never even attempted to have another kid. You can ponder which would be preferable, but, at the end of the day, there is no way to know. Our brains are simultaneously too complex and too simple to process such an extensive, emotional thought. It's just... well... impossible."

I am conflicted in being relieved or saddened that he emphasizes to such a personal degree. I feel like it would be selfish of me to be anything but sad at this point. Evan keeps talking. "Please, don't say you are crazy, June. Please take where we are into account. Think about the people we speak to on a day to day basis… the thing is, I don't even think they are crazy.

"We all have the same potential to go too far mentally or to never venture at all. I think it is a heck of a lot more admirable to think too much than to be shallow.  Honest to God June, I think you are the epitome of sane. You have enough sense to function on a deeper level, but enough strength to hold onto reality."

That was the most meaningful compliment I had ever been paid. The genuine way Evan said it as if it was an undoubted fact, made his statement vivid with validation. *Wow the dead sibling really garnered that 5%.* "Evan, I am so in love with you. Like, help you bury a body under the floorboards kind of love."

Evan and I start with a soft kiss; a tender, loving kiss; *a kiss that makes me thankful to be on the pill.* Then, as his palms cup my face, his open mouth meets mine with intensity, the intertwining of his tongue to mine generates a tingle that surges down my spine. A tingle that abounds to an illustrious level, saturated with longing. With every touch, every press of the lips, every caress, our passion multiplies. I peel his scrub top off effortlessly. He pulls mine over my tangled hair, his wet lips brushing light pecks across my chest and stomach as he lowers to my waist, proceeding to slide off the last of my scrubs. My thumb runs teasingly along the elastic waistband of his pants, before guiding the cloth away from his tan skin.

I ignore a fleeting twinge of embarrassment as I notice my cyan bra does not match my tiger-printed panties. The feverish look in my richly blue eyes encourages Evan to remove them. My hand hovers anxiously at the thought of slipping it under his plaid boxers. Evan seems to sense my hesitation and gently guides my hand to its intended destination.

My animalistic instinct immediately surfaces. Before I know it, his underwear has joined mine on the tiled floor. I brace myself for discomfort as he enters me but am relieved when the feeling of pain is mild, within moments, it dwindles into nonexistence.

The way Evan clutches my heated body close to his soft skin makes me feel secure. I shudder as his silky-lips graze my bare neck. His emerald eyes lock with my sapphire ones, and I bask in the warm glow of light, radiating from our adoring hearts.

When Evan comes, he bites his lip to prevent the sound from escaping the surrounding walls. I feel a wave of gratification knowing I have made somebody feel such captivating pleasure. The experience was not awkward or overwhelming, as I had always anticipated losing my virginity would be. I am happier than I have been in years, maybe ever. Even if I am lying in a shock-therapy-treatment bed.

For once, it is not about Elizabeth in any shape or form. This is my moment. I relish in that. It feels freeing. This act, purely being centered around me, is almost impossible to process. I am grappling at the concept of nobody, but me and a guy my family has never met, not only having sex but being in love.

I have become immersed within an alternate

world. I have developed into my own person and am living apart from everyone I have known for the past eighteen years. I was not even aware that I am capable of such, so the knowledge that I have crafted a fresh life has surpassed me until this precise moment. I am fully conscious of the fact that this internship and lifestyle is not built to last. To me, that is irrelevant. This is just a representation that I, June Wilson, possess the ability to thrive on my own terms.

As I lay there, allowing these thoughts to engross me, I come to a much needed, further realization. My life will always be about me. That is something nobody, no matter how close to you they are, can take away. The only thing that truly defines you is your actions and your feelings. It was immature, in fact downright ridiculous, of me to ever feel otherwise. I cannot loath Lizzie for overriding my life, because that was impossible. A weight lifts from my body as I then understand that it is okay to hate her in a way. Sometimes, it is hard to grasp how deeply you love a person until you hate them on some level. At the end of the day, I know, without a doubt, that I can never hate my sister for dying as much as I love her for living.

*Wow, this night would have been a lot different if I had been on my period.*

# CHAPTER EIGHTEEN: DISTRESSED

When I was eleven, I learned how to slit my wrists. I never did, but I knew how. Our school hosted a seminar about it. The focus was to raise awareness on signs that somebody you know is hurting. The guest speaker had slit his wrists when he was seventeen. He even showed us the jagged scars. He described to us how he took a fresh razor blade out of a brand-new box. How he tested the sharpness of the blade on his palm before realizing the quality to be more than sufficient. The man told us how he forcibly held the razor to his wrist and dragged it along the vein. I remember him saying that cutting sideways does not work. You must slash vertically.

He described to us how hard you must push the razor, and that copious amounts of blood are destined to squirt out. A water fountain being his example. He mentioned that it was incredibly difficult to finish the second wrist before passing out. Not only was the pain unbearable, but the loss of blood caused severe lightheadedness. His final words to me and my classmates were, "Sometimes your family finds you in time. Sometimes your body is slowly drained until your face feels numb, and your breathing comes to a raspy, indefinite stop." *My school got an exceptional number of complaints after this seminar.*

After we have sex, Evan dips into a light lull. Eventually, I begin to dwindle into unconsciousness myself. Peace flows through my body. I welcome the gushing euphoria with gratitude as my eyes begin to close.

Two minutes later, an earsplitting, mechanical-screeching-sound slices the silent air. The high-pitched, mind-numbing noise projects from tiny devices scattered throughout the building. It takes me a moment, or twenty, to fully resurface into reality. I soon realize the unexpected disturbance is caused by the activation of the institution's panic button.

As I hop off the hospital bed and onto my feet, I try to remember if the alert means lockdown, or evacuation, or neither. I also wonder if this is a useless drill or an actual emergency.

Evan is now beside me, as I feel his hand resting on the small of my back. I turn and see that his expression looks as bewildered as I feel.

"What in the world is going on?" His tired voice yells.

I do not respond due to the fact that I am already set into motion. I run out into the hall and see people sprinting to the stairs/elevator. I propel myself through the crowd and up the stairwell. As I bound the steps two-at-a-time, I realize we were heading to the floor housing the patient rooms. A sudden sense of dread begins to swell in my stomach. I force my fatigued legs to quicken, feel myself shoving people harder. My mind is processing so many thoughts it is almost blank. Like when you are flipping through TV channels and go too far. The screen blurs into specks of white and black. I always refer to it as ants fighting. There is so much going on, but nothing is coming together.

I dislike saying that I know something is wrong before the situation is confirmed because it sounds like a placebo effect. I swear, right now, I feel a sinister premonition creeping up my dry throat. That type of feeling has a certain tightness to it. It feels like when you are exercising and hit your breaking point. The point where you can stop and retreat back to your cookies, or you can push yourself to the next level. Though I am running, I definitely feel closer to my breaking point then I should.

A part of me considers reversing back down the stairs to find a safe haven. Wait the ensuing madness out. Maybe I want to put off dealing with the actual problem because I know it is most likely horrible, or perhaps because I am trying to manipulate myself into believing this situation is an overreaction. A dramatizing protocol. Unfortunately, I do not indulge that option for half a second. I trudge on, desperately trying to suck air into my winded lungs.

I suddenly feel my body smash into a hard, yet

slightly mushy, mass. I have been engulfed so deeply in my own panic, that I have run full-force into the mob forming on the outskirts of a patient's room.

I feel my body repel as it crashes into somebody's firm back. My body hits the floor with such an impact that my feet roll completely over my head. I hear a crack and experience a surge of excruciation as somebody unintentionally stomps my delicate pinky finger. I feel several legs rustle the outer edges of my shoulders. Attempting to gather at least one valid thought, I desperately fumble the air, searching for someone, or something to pull me up. I feel hands slip under my arms, yanking me into a standing position. I turn, expecting to see Evan, but am startled to see Victoria's distinctively solemn face melting in woe. I know by her facial expression, that her persistent bitchiness has been overthrown by genuine concern. She too is staggered by whatever is stirring up such a charade.

I throw her a quick thanks as she tugs my arm forward and into the buzzing crowd.

My fearful eyes scan the hall. I read the room numbers, attempting to decipher whose room we are flocking. Honestly, with a mind convoluted by stressful shockwaves, I can barely access my memory enough to recall where I am at all. *Okay, we came from the stairs. I turned right. No, no left. Yeah left. Uh, that makes it the first hall of the left wing, and it's uh five doors down. I know who lives here. I swear, I…*My thoughts are abruptly cut off by a hulking gasp, sounding from my own chest.

The next moments are filled with me slinging elbows and knocking bystanders to the ground. I am focused on finding a way to claw and manipulate myself into that room, no matter the degree of ferocity.

I feel the blood running through my veins freeze like water drizzled into liquid nitrogen. I finally force my way into the room. There, I am met with the most disturbing scene fathomable. No police have yet arrived. Michael is standing there, the amount of salty sweat soaking him gives the illusion that an invisible shower is pouring down. He and a handful of muscular workers are flanking a suspended object. Like children at a birthday party, crowding a pinata. All are trying to pull Randall down from the ceiling fan, where he spins in suffocation, hung by a crimson necktie. His empty eyes are half open, frozen in time. *He is gone.*

Michael sees me hyperventilating in the doorway. "June! Don't look!"

"No!" I shriek hysterically, disregarding Michael in full. I rush to Randall and jerk at his stiff legs, screaming my voice into hoarseness. "Randall, they said you could leave! It just got approved. It's okay, they said you can go home now. Just come back, Randall. I'll drive you, just come back!"

I begin to frantically choke over my tears as Randall's wintry skin remains rigid. I feel Michael's arms wrap around my waist, as he attempts to pry me away from the traumatizing scene. I kick and thrash wildly, but Michael is stronger than he appears.

"June, sweetie, the police are on their way. You cannot be in here. I'm so sorry, June. I am so so sorry." Michael whispers, fighting his own sorrow. He sets me down at the border of the room. I see a severe shiver shake his slender shoulders as he turns back to help the others.

My extremities begin tingling unbearably. My vision blurs to see doubles, no triples. My throat becomes inflamed by the hot vomit launching from my twisted stomach. I stumble in slight before dropping like a swatted fly. The last thought flashing through my mind as my head smacks into the linoleum? *Are you fucking kidding me.*

# CHAPTER NINETEEN:
# RATTLED


I wake up concaved in a murky confusion. My fluttering eyelids feel like dead weights. With every strenuous blink, the room I am in becomes less familiar. I know my head is propped up on a pillow but, from the amount of sharp pain encasing my skull, it might as well be a serrated rock. *Beeping.* That is the first sound to supply my mind with a sense of awareness. Startled by the strange noise, my fingers fly to my lips. A puddle of fresh, gooey drool greets them. I glance down to realize my hand, now glazed with saliva, is adorned with IV's and bandages, a new bracelet wrapped around my right wrist. I am not really a jewelry girl, but I will make an exception for this laminated ring of paper that has my name printed on it. *Seems kind of important.*

I can tell I am in a hospital bed. What hospital?

*No clue.* Why am I here? *Not sure.* Is anybody I know here to be with me? *God, I hope so.*

A few minutes drift by before a young nurse enters my little cell with purpose. "I would greet you with a cutesy saying but you are not a five-year-old waking up from a nap. So, I'll just ask ya how you feel." I stare back at her in silent apprehension, willing her to continue speaking. Telepathically begging her not to make me think with this massive of a headache.

"Not good, huh? Well, we are about to take you on up to CT, make sure you didn't knock anything too hard." She informs me while shining the brightest of lights into my timid eyes. "I'm Danielle. I'm going to be your girl for a little while." She offers a half-smile.

"A few of your friends are here. I think two went for coffee, and one is in the bathroom. Forgive me, I can't quite remember their names. Your family is on the way. They should be here soon." Danielle assures me. I feel a rush of relief.

"I'll be back with your doctor shortly. We'll bring you up to CT. Just push that little blue button to your right if you need anything in the next few minutes. See you soon." Danielle saunters out, an appropriately cheerful smile glued to her face.

Victoria replaces her. She sits down to my left and looks me straight in the eye. Hers are red and puffy. Mine are undoubtedly worse. She leans forward and partially opens her mouth, as if to say something, before reeling back. She is void of words. I know that whatever happened, whatever I will soon remember, is drenched in catastrophe.

From the moment I awoke, I have felt dread gnawing at my mind. I am grateful for this amnesia period because once my brain surfaces the memory of my trauma, the pain is going to burn like blackening frostbite. It will sting relentlessly, and probably leave a part of me feeling dead.

Victoria and I are alone briefly before Evan and Lacey tiptoe into my sterile environment. Their afflicted expressions portray grief, making my heart feel like it is drowning in a vat of quicksand. Evan drags a chair close to the upper part of my bed. He combs his trembling fingers through my knotted hair. The level of heightened worry blaring from his eyes morphs their shade into a darker green. "How are you?"

I am a little stunned to be greeted by Evan as something other than 'Juney' or 'Juney-E.' *Serious times must be upon us*. He begins to softly rub my lower arm. His touch initiates chill bumps to sprout along my body, as it encourages a memory to flash across my eyes.

Leaving his embrace in the shock therapy room, tripping over my own speed as I dashed into the hallway. I also knew Evan was not the reason I was here. He did not beat me into this hospital bed or drive me to a state of psychological frenzy. That post-sex touch was the last I had felt of his until just now.

Victoria, on the other hand, provided me with more insight. She had not sparked a recollection by walking in, but just now she had thanked Lacey for a Styrofoam cup of coffee. I am reminded by her voice. I jolt slightly, hitting the bottom of the cup with my big toe, coercing a few drops into spoiling the thin blanket draped across my feet. I recall her grip helping me off the ground before I could fully be stampeded across. A crack sounds within my mind. I gaze down at my pinky. It is wrapped and splinted.

That is not why I am here though. A finger break is minor. Plus, my head is heavier than a sack of potatoes. I know Victoria pulled me up before anybody had the opportunity to kick it in. I shift my focus to Lacey, wondering if her presence will offer me the clues necessary to solve this puzzle. The anxious expectancy of incoming pain is becoming much too high to fight. I look at Lacey and, at first, see nothing. I have no recollection of her involvement. Then she smiles kindly at me. That unique kindness reminds me of somebody else. With a sharp, abrasive inhale I connect the dots.

*Randall.*

My parents hurry in, just in time to witness my mind weave together a slew of disbelief, heartache, and exasperation. The memory of the insidious event has finally become painstakingly clear.

"Oh no." I murmur, drawing everybody's attention. I try to prevent the flood for but a moment more. Make a stab at building a dam in my eyes for just a brief second. I cannot.

I glance up, a quiver consumes my lips, my tone becomes riddled with panic. "Mommy?"

My parents hug either side of me as water clouds my vision and agonizing wails boom from my body. For the first time in years, I feel close to my mother and father.

After I have hollered and exhausted distraught emotions for a solid half-hour, I am whisked away for a CT. Upon my return, I realize my parents did not come alone. My sisters, Addison and Delilah, are here as well. Plus, my brother-in-law and stepmother. Their presence swiftly transitions from supportive to awkward. I am trying to process. Having the whole lot seems unnecessary because they did not know Randall or the deep, raw sadness his passing burns into my heart. My hospitalization develops into a bizarre family reunion with new additions like charismatic Evan, trying to make a good impression, and spunky Lacey, who Addison immediately adores. I eventually have to request a little time alone.

Addison is reluctant in fulfilling my want. Her reaction is understandable since I dealt with such extensive anxiety issues in the wake of Elizabeth's death. After a few moments though, she seems to comprehend that this situation is different. One, I am older. Two, Randall was somebody I respected and really cared about, but not somebody I had been living with for all my life like my sister. The group shuffles out. Evan is the last person to reach the door. He looks at me, his eyes asking if I want just him to stay. My responding look lets him know that I need a minute to reflect, truly solo.

There I sit in that moderately comfortable bed. I stare up at the bright fluorescent panel hovering above me. I close my eyes and flatten my body as I yank the bed's sheets over my head. I feel secure beneath the papery cloth. Like I am a little girl again, trying to read a book with a flashlight, blocking out the surrounding world's craze.

I feel a sense of fear under the covers, just as I did when I was a child. Fear that my parents would catch me up late, fear that a monster was living within the blanket's crevice, fear that the covers would suffocate me. I think about how much fear Randall felt every, single day. How trapped he was, and how scared that made him.

I consider how terrified Randall had to have been of losing his sanity completely or never being able to regain a sense of comfort. As I resurface under the glowing light, I wonder if he feels relief now. Even if he feels nothing, is that still relief for him? I chose to believe it is because that is the only way I can find some relief from the breath-stealing grief coursing through me.

My solitude lasts less than five minutes. Soon my mother returns to the room. "Hey, hun. We are going to be staying for the funeral. I reserved a hotel room over the phone and brought you some clothes to wear to Raymond's arrangements."

I wince at her mistake but am grateful for her effort. "It's Randall mom, but thank you so much. I really appreciate that."

My CT scans return spotless. The doctor advises that I be prepared for discharge.

"Do you want me to send Addy for your things, June?" My mom asks.

Her question catches me off guard. "Why aren't I staying at Maze?"

My mother looks at me, obviously a tad confused. "You would want to go back there, June? After all of this?"

I love Maze. Maze did not kill Randall, society and war did. Maze housed good people like Michael, Lacey, Pearl, Thomas (ehhh), and most importantly my boyfriend. "I have some things I need to straighten out there, mom. I'll be fine."

"Okay. Well, if you change your mind, I want you to call me or Addy. Alright?" As I nod, I watch her gaze wander over to look upon Evan, who is now standing on the other side of the emergency room curtain, his silhouette visible through the thin fabric. *Hello, hot creeper.*

She turns to face me. The most minuscule hint of a smile plays across her full lips. "I'll let him know he's driving you back. He's a sweetheart, June. I wish he had been in your life a long time ago." *Oh, trust me, homegirl. Me too.*

Addison ends up being the one to chauffeur my wheelchair to the hospital's exit, as Evan pulls around his rental car. Of course, she has to bring up the subject I am mentally avoiding. "So, Evan's cute. Guess you will be making some trips to Colorado, then?"

I force a synthetic grin at her, unsure of how else to react. Evan and I are unstable, our relationship imminently platonic.

As I crack open the car door, the fog of tense air consuming the environment of Evan's car hits my emotions head-on. My eyes avoid contact with his as I slide in. The passenger-side mirror catches in my peripheral vision, offering my mother's approaching reflection. She jogs along the oatmeal-colored concrete, a neon orange beach bag swinging in her left hand.

"June!" My mom calls out as she meets the window. Evan jumps in alarm before rolling it down quickly.

"June," she repeats, out of breath. "These are some clothes for you to wear the next couple of days." Her panting finally ceases. She is able to stand up straight, her voice stabilizing with normal inflection.

"I brought you a couple of dresses, some from Lizzie's service. Hopefully, everything still fits. You know you looked so pretty in them." The last sentence causes her caramel irises to dampen.

I then say something she is not expecting. "Thanks. I love you very much, mom."

As we trudge back to Maze, Evan is a phantom of himself. The drained boy is almost unrecognizable. His usually warm, inviting demeanor, is replaced with a frigid, stressed aura. Aware that we have extensive conversational ground to cover. We need to talk about Randall, Maze, us. These impending discussions muting to the point where I am scared to utter a single word. I do not even have the courage to ask him to switch the radio station to something other than static. His pale lips look cemented to one another.

A little ray of light shines into the vehicle as I set my hand down, palm up, on the middle consult. He cautiously takes one hand off of the wheel and interlocks his fingers with mine. As we drive, his grip tightens to a painful extent. I find reassurance in this pain. We may have been thinking about the same thing, or be having completely unrelated thoughts, but at least we are still holding onto a piece of one another, firmly.

When his car pulls into Maze, I feel moisture abandon my mouth and constriction seize my throat. I remember the first day my tires rolled over this dusty, uneven parking lot. I recall awkwardly waving at the patients in the lawn. I think about how unnerved I felt as they gazed back at me. I now feel overwrought with shame for that reaction. The patients are not scary, they are not unruly, and most of all, they are not test subjects. They are humans, good people, trapped in a dark cave that only they can see.

When I walked up the steps at Maze a couple of months ago, it seemed to have vibrant color in its bricks, cleanliness in its white trimmings, and openness in its large windows. I recall thinking *Wow does an asylum really have to be so nice? It's a mental institution for crying out loud.*

Today, I can see the dilapidated roof sinking in, the beige streaks along the worn brick, the dingy color of the trimmings, the lack of clarity in the massive windows, and even the excessive overgrowth eating at the stairs. All the faults I neglected.

The sweet patients, the hardworking employees, even the cocky doctors, they all deserve so much more. I feel tears brewing as Evan and I pass through the door. Inside, I feel disgustingly wrong and certifiably guilty for any negative assumptions I made toward the people who are simply trying to fabricate a life at Maze.

Michael is sitting on a sofa chair in the corner of the foyer, reading a book, his eyes ghostly. As the sturdy door slams behind us, I notice Michael's face falter while simultaneously filling with relief. He gets up and walks towards me, sweeping me into a hug. We both squeeze each other as tears glide down his face, and I sob into his bony shoulder. He starts murmuring, "I'm so sorry you had to see that June. I am so sorry you got hurt too."

I steady my fluttering breath in order to obtain an ounce of control over my tuckered-out emotions. I thank Michael for attempting to shield me from the horror. He chews his bottom lip in response. I am sure, in his opinion, he was unable to. I still saw Randall. I even jerked at his lifeless corpse. However, Michael was not responsible for that in the least. He had tried to reason with me. That is the best he could have done.

Silence sets in for a few moments until Evan asks, "how are you, Michael?"

"I'm devastated," he mumbles. "We all are."

# CHAPTER TWENTY: ANXIOUS

"Well... What the Hell do you want to do June?" inquires Evan, once we are settled back into my room. I have been staring outside my tiny window. The parking lot has been my view for the entirety of my stay. Dusk is now overthrowing day, the last glimmer of twilight fading into darkness. I was aware this question was coming, but it still catches me off guard.

"I mean I would suggest dinner, but I'm pretty full from that delectable, oh-so-runny hospital Jell-O," I divert. I know exactly what he means, but comedic suppression is really outweighing mature conversation right now. *Shocker.*

I turn away from the dimming view, plopping down on my bed's bouncy corner. Evan is lounging across. I guide his bare feet to my lap and begin to rub them gently, resisting the innate urge to tickle.

"Juneyyy.." he pleads. I am reluctant to give in to Evan's want, that being to debate our future.

What is going to become of our fun, quirky relationship in just three short days.

My mouth remains wordless as I rest my head on his extended right arm. My tongue glosses the soft-skin of my quivering lips before allowing their dewiness to crash into his. I persist in my pursuit, every taste of Evan's sweet breath making me feel closer to safety. The oversized T-shirt and cotton panties I had slipped on are gliding right back off, becoming lost in my tangled sheets. He touches me with less caution this time, making my toes curl in pulsating pleasure before he is even in me. I need him to look at me in the eyes as his legs straddle my thighs, I need his vibrant irises to promise me security. But his lids remain shut. So, I close mine as well, letting the intense sensations overwhelm my mental uncertainty. I soon become lost in the rapture of our mingling skin, the naturality of our movement distracting my thoughts in full. I feel closer to Evan then I have ever felt to anybody, for that half hour at least. *Yeah half-hour. Not bad for eighteen.*

His eyes only open to roll back in satisfaction. As soon as his orgasm finishes, I shove him off of me and begin searching for my discarded underwear. I cannot find them anywhere. I tear up the sheets and check under the bed. I start to become frantic. Before I know it, shallow breaths are sounding from my tired lungs, and hot water is pouring from my exhausted eyes. *Daisy with Gatsby's shirts.*

Evan is baffled. "June what's wrong? Honey, it's okay. I'll find them Juney, it's okay." Except nothing is okay. I freeze in the bed, my hands shaking atop the covers like leaves rustling in the breeze.

"Evan… We can't..." I begin to stutter but am rudely interrupted by my own whimpers and sniffles.

"June, it's alright. Just lay down with me for a minute. I've got you." Evan assures as he guides my trembling shoulders back to the mattress.

I cling to him as I try to stabilize my sanity. Once he considers me calm enough, Evan completes what I had started to say. "June, I know we are young. I know long distance is difficult. I know this is an appropriate time for us to embrace a fresh start, but I do love you, Juney. If you want to try, we will try, because I care about you so much. You may be the snidest girl I have ever met, but you are compassionate. Even if you are blind to it. You helped Randall. You helped all the patients here just by being the one thing people rarely are to them: kind. I will try my absolute hardest to make this work if it's what you want. I swear. Do you think we can do it June?"

I bite the inside of my cheek, waiting for the taste of salty blood to invade my mouth, before answering with a heart-breaking, but definitive, "no."

The truth? Evan is perfect. I wish we were in our late twenties. I wish we would have met at a coffee shop, or a cock-fight, or in any other setting. In all honesty, I had been planning to pursue long distance with Evan. Over the past few weeks the idea had really grown on me, and I was terrified to hear his thoughts on the situation. Now though, I need the fresh start he mentioned. There is still so much sadness in my heart over the loss of my sister, and now with the knowledge of Randall's death, that melancholy feeling has multiplied. I have to start at Auburn in the fall, and I have to do it alone.

"Evan?" I know he deserves an elaboration but touching more on this heinous subject feels like chomping down on a bag of jagged glass.

"Yes?" He responds without hesitation.

"We are not ready to pursue this. It will cause stress. We will be absolutely miserable not being able to see one another. It could distract us from forming real bonds at college. We might end up resenting each other. Long distance will guarantee our breakup, so let's not drag it out." He nods in agreement, but his face is now crumbling.

"Can you promise me one thing?" I continue. "If I was to show up in Avon about five years from now, will you teach me how to ski?"

At this, he releases a melodious chuckle. The sound instantly makes my heart feel a million times lighter. "I am not a miracle worker, but I will definitely teach you how to keep your face from smacking the snow."

Then I ruin the tender moment because I suffer from unyieldingly inappropriate personality traits. "Maybe you knocked me up, and we'll feel obligated to stay together!"

## CHAPTER TWENTY-ONE: BEYOND ALL REASON

I awake the following morning with a head heavier than a sack of flour. The idea of getting up and starting the day seems unbearable. When my sister died, people told me I was *so strong*. Strength is a façade. You get through the unimaginable scenarios because you have to. You just do it. There is no set of skills to be strong. As long as you avoid suicide and being locked in a mental institution, you are technically being strong. However, in this scenario, the convenience of already being at an asylum is awfully tempting.

This morning though, I have somewhere to be. I yank some recently-washed pink scrubs out of my laundry basket and pull them on. I step into my once white, but now ivory with dust and dirt, colored sneakers for the last time. I dread making eye contact with my reflection as I enter my quaint bathroom. I am being foolish. Yes, the skin surrounding my eyes is swollen, and scarlet, and I look like a drug addict who has just killed a puppy, but all of that is temporary. I brush a reluctant comb through my knotted hair before gathering the copper strands up into a tight ponytail.

I leave my room, still wearing my name tag, and head to the cafeteria like I do every morning. I dodge the food line and instead go straight to the hulking espresso machine. Once I am standing in front of the shiny metal, it occurs to me that this contraption is complex beyond my comprehension. I am not sophisticated like Randall. So, I slide over to the worn coffee pot cowering in its shadow. I pour myself a cup and add hazelnut flavored creamer to it because I could always detect that smell wafting from Randall's mug.

I snatch a petite cream cheese Danish before setting off to be with my friend. I sit there in the rocker he consistently used and gaze out at the vast forest consuming the edges of Maze Estates. The trees appear more vibrant today and, despite the sweltering heat, the plants seem rejuvenated with life. I curl up with my steaming coffee, pulling one leg up and tucking it beneath the other. I let my big toe drag across the carpet to prevent my back and forth motion from stopping. I feel swathed in calm bliss.

The images of Randall's death, the hollowness of his eyes, haunt me. The memories of talking to him here; they lessen the frequency of these visions. I may have been pulling air in and pushing it back out of my lungs nonstop, but for the first time since I saw Randall's body, I can breathe.

I jump a little when I feel a hand atop my head. I look up, startled, and see one of God's most well-done jobs. I give the Lord a metaphorical high-five as Evan sits beside me. He takes my hand to hold on his lap, running his thumb soothingly across my knuckles.

"Sorry I left you this morning, June. I just knew I was scheduled to sit in with Pearl and Dr. Mosh this morning. I could not bear to lose one final session with her. She has been so sweet to me. I mean I think she was trying to seduce me, but still, I had to say goodbye." He says as his eyes ingest our view. I understand completely. I wish I could have had the same opportunity with my favorite patient.

"How'd you know I was here?" I inquire.

"Because Randall is here." He replies.

I sip my drink in peace as Evan rocks beside me, engrossed in thought. I draw comfort from his quiet presence. Eventually, he reminds me of the time. We go back to my room to get properly dressed.

We shower together for the first time. It feels totally odd at first. I have not bathed with somebody since my siblings and I were toddlers. I have to request that the lights be off because I always shower in the dark.

Evan is taken aback by my request, but he agrees saying, "as long as nobody gets head-butted." I laugh and am grateful to be granted the serenity I crave. *Until he maliciously turns the water to a sub-zero temperature.*

Today is Randall's viewing. I wear the dress I wore on the second day of Elizabeth's arrangements. Elizabeth had a two-day viewing because her body was still in decent condition, or at least the mortician made it appear to be. I am sure Randall's neck is now mangled and indented by a raw, red scar. No matter how much makeup they layered on him, everybody would still know it is there. His casket is closed, which comes as a relief to me, and I am sure to anyone else aware of the circumstances.

Evan and I are intercepted by Lacey the moment we hobble into the cramped parlor. As I listen to Lacey talk, tears infecting her voice, I cannot help but become distracted. In the corner of my eye, I have caught a glimpse of a woman with these intensely blue eyes. The kind of eyes that appear icy because they are so pale and appear razor-sharp. They are eyes that belong to somebody intelligent. They are Randall's eyes.

My gaze zooms over to get a complete look at the lady. Her eyes seem even brighter in contrast with the red blotches surrounding them. She appears youthful in a way, but the beginning traces of wrinkles and the few strands of gray in her otherwise vibrantly blonde hair make me think she is middle-aged. I know within an instance that she is Randall's mother.

Randall's mom is standing beside her son's sealed coffin, a soaked handkerchief clenched in her quaking hand. People surround her, yet she seems isolated. I resonate with her because that is precisely how I felt at Elizabeth's viewing. At the time I was grateful so many people cared about my sister, but mentally I was underwater. Everything sounded muffled, nobody was able to guide me back to the surface.

In a twisted, completely self-indulgent way, I am thankful to not be her. Seeing the pain in her eyes feels chilling as it brings me back to the horror of Elizabeth's passing. Though I am heartbroken and traumatized over Randall's death, at least I am not a member of the deceased one's family this time. As sad as his death makes me feel, they are the ones being tortured. I know firsthand just how gut-wrenching that feels.

Not too long after I realize who the woman is, I am shuffled into a line that ends in the offering of condolences to her, Randall's father, brother, and sister. I am caught off-guard when I start to introduce myself to them, and his mother, Marie, interrupts me. "You said June? That's your name?"

My lips twitch shyly before answering. "Yes, ma'am. I was an intern here this summer." *Here? Yeah forgot to mention that I have actually been working at the funeral home.* "I mean Maze." I catch myself. "I interned at Maze Estates."

Marie shows a glimmer of a smile in her eyes as she responds. "Honey, I came to visit my baby a few weeks ago. He said 'mom I am getting along famously with one of the interns this year. Her name is June. She's so bright, and it makes me feel like Kara is here with me.'"

She begins getting choked up as she ushers a teenager, who could have easily been Marie's twin, in front of her. "June, I'd like you to meet Kara. This is Randall's little sister. They were, are, very close. She's only fifteen, can't drive so he didn't get to see her as much as we would have wanted."

I look at Kara and try so hard to resist falling apart. The poor girl. She is not much older than I was when I lost my own sibling.

"It meant so much to us." Marie continues as I stare at Randall's sister. I grab Kara and hug her tightly, before turning to Marie and doing the same. I manage to say, "I know I did not know him for long, but Randall will always be one of my favorite people. I'm so, so sorry to all of you," before breaking down. I move out of the way so that the people behind me, who Randall's life touched in some way, can honor his memory.

My left-hand glides lightly over the sleek coffin, I twiddle with a little blue forget-me-not nestled into the flower arrangement atop it. My cautious eyes swoop the perimeter before picking it and walking away. The blossom resting in the safety of my palm, I know that no matter how hard today is, tomorrow will be worse. *I should write inspirational quotes for a living.*

# CHAPTER TWENTY-TWO: DERANGED

I am relieved to still be nestled within Evan's warm embrace the next morning. My palm smacks my alarm clock hard when it wakes me from a shallow, recently-achieved slumber. I want Evan to be woken up by me, his *pleasant* girlfriend, not a horribly obnoxious beeping noise. Cheesy as it sounds, I have always wanted to wake somebody up with kisses. My parents told me that when I was a baby, and Lizzie was four, she would try to wake me up from a nap by planting big, slobbery kisses all over my chubby face. Apparently, it was cute at first, but it got to the point where my naps were being interrupted consistently. So, she got in a little trouble and was told to stop.

I was lying in bed one night, probably a year after Elizabeth had died, and I decided when I grow up and have a family, everybody will be awoken by kisses every morning. Elizabeth had always been the most affectionate person in my family. After she was gone, I realized how important sharing affection with loved ones truly is. I took it for granted recklessly. I attempted to start the trend early by waking up my cats with this strategy. They remain unamused.

I creepily observe Evan's sleep for a moment, hearing his steady, easy breathing feels assuring. I would have listened to it for a few more minutes, but unfortunately, I have to pounce prematurely when a flicker of his eyelid makes me think he is waking up. I ambush that boy with what I estimate to be a thousand pecks.

A smile consumes both his lips and eyes. His fingers try to tickle me in defense before stopping and holding my face to his. He gives me the most passionate, heart-warming kiss of all time. His quality certainly beating my quantity.

After Evan's lips release mine, we both sigh deeply before pulling ourselves out from under the cozy blankets. I want to look nice at Randall's funeral. Not for vain reasons. It just feels necessary to look respectable for such a ceremony. Today is the last event dedicated solely to Randall.

I cringe at the thought of my wavy hair hanging in my face like usual. I pull it up and am even able to twist it, before fastening the look with a couple pins. The style actually appears elegant. I coat my eyelashes with the waterproof mascara my aunts got me for Lizzie's funeral. It is hard to imagine any makeup being truly able to withstand water, but it seemed to work that day, and God knows I put that cosmetic to the test. *Hopefully, I do not get an infection from the fact that it is four years old.* I even try to elevate my face by borrowing a tube of burgundy lipstick from Addison.

As I am painting my lips with the paste that seems to be eucalyptus and dirty bath water scented, I hear Evan, who is in my bedroom, mumbling, presumably at me. "It feels weird that Randall's service will be military. Just didn't seem like a part of his life anymore."

Nausea creeps into my stomach as I react to Evan's reminder. In my opinion, the people overseeing Randall's treatment failed him tremendously. It is not the military's fault. I know all they do is protect us. The government though, that is a much different, and scarily convoluted, story. The people involved in Randall's situation are corrupt; I know it.

I make an effort in shoving this information out of my mind as I walk out of my bathroom to get dressed. I go to the bag my mother had slung dresses into and pull one out at random. I unfold the gown and realize it is the dress I wore to Elizabeth's service. I know the flowy, ballerina resembling gown had looked gorgeous on me, but today it could not have appeared more repulsively hideous. I shove it back in the bag, offended by its presence. *Insufficient.*

"Hey Evan, do you have scissors in your room?" I ask casually as I slide on a clean pair of lace panties.

"Uh, yeah, Think so. What's up?" He inquires, obviously confused.

"Could you just grab them for me real quick,

hun?" I rummage through my closet to find a black bra. He nods before leaving briefly.

Upon his return. he hands me a pair of seemingly new scissors. *Nice and sharp*. I yank the funeral dress back out of the bag and cut it to shreds, tossing the scraps of cloth into my bathroom's trash can. *Much better*. That dress represents the worst day of my life. Its existence is completely unnecessary.

Evan's sparkling eyes are wide with shock as I skip back into the bedroom. I innocently smile without using my teeth and shrug. I drag the dress I wore to my graduation out of the bag, and swiftly glide over the fabric with an iron I borrowed from Lacey, before putting it on.

I step into some maroon-colored kitten heels and begin to panic. I am ready. Evan is ready. If we do not leave soon, we will be late. It is time to go to Randall's funeral, though I appear to be glued together, I could not feel more torn.

Halfway through Randall's service, I stop being sad, trading the melancholy emotion in for anger. Rage in fact. I glance to the side at Marie, I see the way she clings to her husband who is barely stable himself. The couple looks moments away from toppling on over. I peer across Evan's shoulder to see Kara, her face burrowed deeply in her brother's chest. I turn my gaze on him, defeat blaring from his wet eyes. I notice that the knuckles on the hand he is using to rub his sister's back are purple with scuffed scrapes. Probably punched a wall or two from grief-induced frustration.

In front of me is a man unfolding an American

flag over Randall's casket. I wonder if he ever met Randall. I am sure he had, and that if I had been paying more attention during the earlier parts of the service, I would have known that. I had been distracted though by these two smug-looking women. They were close to the military crowd honoring Randall, but still, they were there separate. The whole service, my eyes felt cemented to them. For some reason, I could not get over their snobby looking faces, though I have no clue who they are, just seeing them agitates my system.

I feel chills run rampant down my spine as my ears ring in the loudest gunshot known to man. The service might be coming to a close, but I still have a mission. Once the funeral is officially over, I spot the two women shaking hands with military folk, a few graves over from Randall's. I venture out after them.

I hear Evan call out behind me. "Juney, where are you going?"

"I'll be back!" I say, without looking over my shoulder.

The women begin stalking towards the parking lot, so I speed up. I trip over and shatter a flower-filled vase on the way. I cannot stop though, determination is propelling me forward.

"Hi!" I holler a few times, my volume increasing with each shout. They continue. It is not until I scream, "ladies!" that they put a halt on their quick stride and turn to face me. Once I reach them, I have to take a breath-catching moment before speaking. *Oh no. What in the world am I even going to say?*

I start out with naïve questions. "I'm sorry to charge you. I just know I've seen y'all before. It is driving me nuts. Could you refresh my memory real quick?" The two professionally dressed, thin, solemn-looking women gape at me like I am a complete maniac. *Maybe I am.*

"Uhhh,'" the younger one stammers, the quick dart of her eyes reveals complete perplexion. "Are you involved at Maze?"

The response that validates my intuition. I knew they were connected to Randall's wellbeing. "Yes! In fact, I am an intern there. Did you ladies visit Randall?"

I can tell my question wounds the older woman's pride because her words snap at me. "No, we were not visitors. We supervised Mr. Creed's evaluations."

*Oh man were my instincts on point.* "Oh, that's right. What a great guy, you know? I'd talk to him, and he'd be so grounded. I was bewildered he even needed to be institutionalized."

The women can sense the snideness seeping out of my tone. From their annoyed, yet somewhat frightened, facial expressions I am positive they can tell I am on to them.

The older woman speaks again, having to clear her throat this time, her gulp visible through the wrinkled skin of her neck. "Randall was very nice. You are young; it is hard to comprehend adult problems, but Mr. Creed was very ill. What happened to him was unfortunate." She attempts to turn on her heels, but my hand latches onto her elbow, forcing her to stay.

"Wow, you are so right. It is unfortunate when people die. *How insightful.* You know, some people, like Randall, feel a lot of guilt when others die. Randall listened, helplessly, to three of his friends be murdered, and the guilt swallowed him. He wanted to be home, with his parents. He wanted to heal." I am not backing down. My words *will* be heard.

"Okay intern, I am glad you know what he wanted. What Mr. Creed needed was treatment. A lot of other people need it too. Which is why our job is very important, and we need to go." Spits back the younger woman, the cat finally letting go of her tongue.

"Okay, fine," I respond. "Go put the nail in some other hero's coffin, so you can bury the secrets they would never tell." My fingers supplying the bitch's elbow with a forceful pinch before releasing it.

I stalk back towards the crowd of Randall's loved ones, leaving the cowards standing next to their car. I feel their shocked glares burning into my back. *The heat feels nice.*

Michael is the first familiar face I see upon returning.

"Hey Michael, can I have a word with you?" Not only is he important in all of Maze's affairs, but he also has a blood relative living there.

"Of course, June. What's up?" Michael follows me over to the shade of a nearby willow.

"Michael, did Randall seem out of control to you?" I ask.

"Not at all, June." He responds swiftly.

"With all the patients you have seen go in and out, how long do they usually stay?" I inquire.

"Well many stay years, but young ones like Randall, maybe a few months? At most? Not going to lie June, but I was always confused when Randall continued to be denied discharge." He offers. Obviously, he knew the direction in which the conversation was headed.

I decide to be blunt. "Why?"

"Well, we have a double evaluation system at Maze. Our doctors decide if a patient is ready to go back into the care of family. Then, I have to process the file by sending it to higher-ups. If there seems to be anything fishy within the files, other psychologists come to Maze to make further evaluations. Usually, it is just a formality. I sent Randall's file quite frequently, in fact, as often as possible. Every time it was flagged. Which is to be expected with his military involvement. The psychologists would come, always the same ones, and deny him. Say he just fell apart during his interview." Michael pauses, staring at the grass beneath us for a moment before continuing.

"If I had not been sending his file for discharge, then they would have never come, June. No check-ups were ever officially scheduled. I feel like they wanted to... I hate saying this, but I feel like they wanted his sanity to rot here." It is clear from the pain behind Michael's honest eyes, that this has been weighing heavily on his chest.

"Michael, I think I'm going to tell his family." He lifts his head in surprise.

"What? June, they can't hear something like

that. Not right now." No matter his response my mind is set.

"Maybe not, but they need to hear it soon," I tell him.

My car is packed and ready to be driven home after the funeral, so I know this will be my last time seeing Michael this summer. I embrace him and thank him for being genuine. I admire Michael. I hope to hold on to a piece of his kindness as I grow older.

Evan comes up behind me just as I am walking towards Marie. His heated arms wrap around my waist, and I glance up at his sullen, but still pleasant, face. "Juney, I'm not ready for us to part yet." He says before planting a kiss on my now sweaty forehead.

"Well good," I respond. "Because Addison's husband is driving my car home. You and I are following him back to Eufaula in your rental. You still have a week before flying out, you are spending it with me. I am going to take you to the best Cajun restaurant in the entire world."

I have been waiting to surprise him with this information. After a purely ecstatic look sweeps across his sun-kissed face, I feel a twinge of guilt for waiting. "I've got to talk to Randall's mom before we leave, okay?"

"Do you want me to come with you?" Evan asks sweetly.

"No hun. This is something I have to do alone."

Evan understands. "Alright. I'm gonna grab Lacey, and we'll wait by the car, so you get to say goodbye to her."

"Thanks," I say before continuing towards Marie. The timing is actually perfect because, for the first time over the past couple of days, she is physically alone. I am not approaching her to voice my concerns about the circumstances of Randall's death. I would have never done that at such a sensitive time.

Marie notices me just as I notice a small, worn-looking stuffed animal clenched in her right fist. It is a rabbit, its fur matted, and its whiskers bent out of shape from years of love. I assume it was Randall's. My heart shatters into pieces smaller than marbles. It feels like fiberglass is nestled deeply into my chest, creating a scorching itch that will never be scratched.

The bunny threw me for a loop. My mind is washed blank. In that moment, I am at an utter loss for words. Despite her grief, Marie has grace in her presence. She squeezes me and kisses me on the cheek as I blubber sorry to her.

"I am so glad you came and gave me the opportunity to meet you." She whispers. Just as she begins to walk away, I recall the one thing I have to ask her.

"Mrs. Creed, wait!" I call before she can get too far. She spins around as I catch up to her. I pull out Evan's mobile that I snatched from his pocket a few minutes ago. *I'll give it back, don't worry.* Mine is just in the car right now.

"Can I have your home number, please? I would really like to talk to you soon." I request.

She seems happy that I thought to ask. "Of course. Anytime, dear."

I watch Marie return to her husband's warm embrace. I see a slender woman, her skin peaches and cream, walking over to the couple. A little girl with cork-screw curls bounces in her arms. I wonder if it is Simon's wife.

A finger taps on my shoulder, and I turn to lock eyes with the one person who truly hurt me at Maze, Victoria. As my heels fight the urge to redirect, I remember how much pain Victoria prevented by helping me off the floor. I think about the genuine look of grief twisting her face, while at the hospital. She pulls me in for an unexpected hug before saying, "I hope this summer humbled you as much as it did me."

I nod and wish her luck with college. As I begin to walk away, she calls out after me. "June! I know you loved your sister." It was not an apology, but it was absolutely enough for me.

I stumble back to find Evan, feeling lost in a daze. I need somebody to guide me. Like in that game you play when you are a kid. You pretend to be blind and your friends lead the way. The whole purpose is to avoid smacking into the wall. Except today, the wall is people, and nobody is here to take my hand.

Then, I hear a distinct princess-like voice rise above the crowd. "Baby doll we are over here!" *Lacey.* I can now see her painted nails waving above the sea of heads. The thought of saying goodbye to Lacey makes my heart-ache. She might be gratuitous at times, but she is caring and spunky, and pleasant without taking lip from anybody. I am going to miss her southern sass to no end.

"Okay sweet girl, I know you're already upset. I'm not going to make you any sadder, okay? You are an absolute joy, June. You are mature, and I know you're shy, but you have so much personality. You just have to let it shine through, baby. You are going to go to college and make so many friends, and hey I'll always be your friend! My hubby loves fishing off of Lee County Lake. Says he always finds the plumpest trout there. We have each other's numbers. I'll go with him one day, pick you up from school, and we will have a little girl's day. How's that sound?" Lacey talks away, chipper as always. *As long as he doesn't make me eat raw meat that'd be great!*

"I would love that! Thank you so much for everything, Lacey. You have been more helpful than you know. Can't wait to see you soon!" She pulls me in for an embrace so tight I feel like a mouse being squeezed to death by a boa constrictor.

That's the day I last saw Maze.

## CHAPTER TWENTY-THREE:
## SHOOK UP

The pain of Randall's death is…. *different.*
Yes, it was traumatizing to see his corpse. Yes, I
know things have to be made right in his honor.
Yes, I want so badly to have morning coffee with
him again. I do not miss him the way I was
expecting to. I thought I would miss him the way I
missed my sister after her death, but I had few
memories with Randall. Mourning him is easier. It
is manageable.

I am able to cherish that week of summer love
with Evan and find the closure I need. We had done
little together, date wise, due to the circumstances
of our internships at Maze. We try to cram as many
fun activities into a week as possible. Well, that was
the idea at least when we talked about it in the car.
In reality, we spent quite a significant amount of
time renting our favorite movies and curling up in
my bed to show one another. We would start getting

ready to go out and then end up talking for hours, totally missing out on our plans. Plus, we are horny teenagers that could not resist one another's touch. It did not matter though. If we lost our dinner reservation a couple of nights, there was always Waffle Mansion. Greasy bacon and overcooked eggs became a romantic staple in our relationship. *Turns out it tastes even better after sex.*

The best part about bringing Evan home was introducing him to my ginger cat, Sir Thomas the III. My parents never told me what happened to the first or the second, but for sanity's sake, I assume they live on a farm with lots of mice to hunt. Tommy Cat, as I call him, is on the heftier side. He is only a couple of years old, but his appetite is as fierce as a tiger. When we got to my house, I immediately ran up the stairs to my bedroom. I squealed with childlike delight when I saw Tommy, snuggled into a ball in the center of my duvet. I coddled, and baby talked to my cat for a minute before scooping him up. I relocated Tommy to my doorway, where Evan stood, laughing uncontrollably.

I offer Tommy's paw, and Evan becomes very solemn. He gives the jelly-bean toes a firm shake. "It's a delight to meet you, Sir." He says before Tommy meowed violently at me, forcing me to set him on the ground unless I wanted to get shanked. Every single time Evan walked into a room, in my house, he had Tommy casually cradled in his right arm. It never failed. He was infatuated with my kitty. Which, as crazy as it seems, meant the world to me.

A triumph of Evan's visit was my return to the lake. My grandparents owned a dock on Walter F. George lake and, even after they died, my family continued to use it. I enjoyed it right up until my sister drowned on the opposite side of the same lake. The water I once thought to be refreshing and fun, became stale and offered me no invitation.

I was always a swimmer growing up, like Randall. I had tried out for my high school swim team in early May of 8th grade. The lake was where I had learned to improve my swim speed and manage my time. My family did not own a pool, so the lake was where I always practiced. I adored it because of its silence. During the summer, my mom or Addison would take me to the dock. I would swim for hours as one of them sat on a beach chair and read a book. I made my high school swim team, even scoring better than most of my future teammates. I was set to start my freshman year of school. I was ready to work hard all summer, in order to be prepared for competition.

Then Elizabeth died. Right in my practice waters. Right as that summer began. The idea of not only getting in that lake but swimming again, made my stomach churn. My mom and Addison tried and tried to make me go back, but I refused. They continued to visit the dock every now and then, but I would not. A part of me felt like I would drown too.

I think my mom told Evan all of this, because the Friday before he left, I woke up to a tote bag, packed with my swimsuit and towels, perched on the corner of my bed. Evan was creepily standing over me in swim trunks and a bright white t-shirt. An eager smile dancing across his face… Still holding my cat.

Evan was… Uh Evan with me when we got to the dock. He pounced right into the water but immediately swam back to talk to me. I fidgeted nervously with my suit strap as I tried dipping so much as a toe in the haunting reservoir. "C'mon Juney-E. I've got you." He assured, before pulling at my legs, flipping me over his shoulder and into the water.

For a moment, I felt smothering panic under the water I had so dread reuniting with. Then, I felt an unexpected surge of peace. A similar peace to the one I felt while having coffee in Randall's rocker. I resurfaced, yelling playfully and began splashing water at Evan, tears streaming from my eyes. I felt happy. I felt brave. *Most of all, I felt relieved.*

Mine and Evan's goodbye was anticlimactic. Evan is not one for drama. After everything that had happened the week before, neither was I. We packed his rental car while telling each other our favorite moments of the summer, per Evan's suggestion. Once his last overnight bag was secured in the back seat, I turned to tell him to be safe. Instead, I am met with the delicious press of his sugary lips. *Damn that pixie stick.* The kiss lingered after his mouthed unhooked from mine, the tingle made me feel loved.

I went in for another kiss, one I held on to so long it put him in danger of missing his flight back to Colorado. Evan slowly began shuffling in reverse to his driver's side door. I knew I had to let go. His fingers slid from my back to grip my hands. He squeezed them tightly. He looked me in the eye, his face wearing the same signature crooked smile I noticed the first day we met. "Thanks for keeping your promise, Juney-E. Glad you kept me from losing my sanity this summer."

# CHAPTER TWENTY-FOUR: OVERWROUGHT

I must forgive Elizabeth. Randall had made that clear. My resentment towards her is stunting my growth as a person. *Even making me bitter.* The problem is that this is way easier said than done. Is there a manual with instructions on how to forgive your sister, who you love, but also called a bitch, who didn't upset you that much when alive, but pissed you off by croaking? Did I miss my funeral handout? After Evan is back in Colorado, I begin making attempts at healing.

First, I watch movies Elizabeth and I had enjoyed together. Though watching them is sentimental, it really just makes me realize we had poor taste, and a raunchy sense of humor, as children. I know she would have felt the same way, which makes my heart feel heavy, as I want to laugh with her about it.

The next day, I approach Delilah. I try to act

like the big sister Elizabeth was to me. I walk into Delilah's room a little after noon. She is sitting criss-cross on the floor, filing her nails, and looking through a magazine that is plastered with pictures of boy bands. I cringe as I realize she is pasting cut-outs of the apostles' faces over those of cheeky singers. *Lord help me.* I am unsure of how to proceed, so I awkwardly stand in the door frame, messing with my ponytail, until she notices me.

Once we make eye contact, I ask, "Heyyyy, Delilah. Is there uh anything you need advice about?"

She simply rolls her eyes and resumes flipping through the magazine, searching for more faces to enlighten. "No." Her tone radiates with teenage angst.

"You sure? Not with like guys, or anything? Are you a Judas girl?" I further-inquire. "I mean he is the ultimate bad boy."

She ignores me.

"Do you want me to do your makeup?" I offer.

"June, I'm not going anywhere, and let's be real, you can barely do your own," Delilah replies.

"Wanna see who can fit the most grapes in their mouth?" I exclaim, becoming desperate.

Delilah sets down her nail file and turns herself to fully face me. "June are you trying to sell me crack?" *Ugh.*

"No," I say, defeated, and offended.

"Good. Can you please stop with the questions, and let me have some private time?" she requests.

"Sure." I slump through our joint-bathroom and back to my bedroom. Obviously, that was a fail.

I take a couple of days off from "forgiving" Lizzie to recuperate. Then, I get weird. A few nights after my try with Delilah, I decide to go old school. Around three in the morning, witching hour, I ignite some candles in my room and turn off the lights. The intertwined scent of vanilla cupcake, peony, and pine needle wax is putrid, but those were what I could find around the house. I pull out the Ouija board hidden in the closet of my mom's office. Her and my dad got freaky in the late seventies. *Go figure.*

I bring the game into my room and sit on the floor, a fuzzy throw blanket over my head. I realize I have no clue how to even work a Ouija board. I just start murmuring. "Lizzie if you're out there, I'm sorry. I'm sorry for being so mad at you."

*Oh my God.* I freeze as I hear a creak outside my door. My muscles tense. The hairs on my arms stand like ballerinas on point as the sound of soft thuds approach me.

"Lizzie…?" I whisper, utterly terrified. I scream and rip off the blanket as I feel something brush against me.

"Oh." Relief washes through me. "Hi, Sir Thomas. We need to go to bed. And we need to stop with the scary movies."

Turns out, I do end up being right about one thing. Delilah is going to help me forgive Elizabeth.

A couple of days after I went spooky, and a week before I left for school, I catch Delilah watching some out-of-the-ordinary film in not her room, but mine. *Wait that sounded off, I don't mean porn.* She scares me half to death as I come out of the bathroom, not an ounce of cloth on my body, and see her sitting on the carpet.

She is as close to my television as the stand underneath it will allow her. The crimson rim around her eyes indicates crying. I remain in a state of bewilderment as I ravage my closet for something to cover my indecency. I have no clue why she is not watching her own equally sufficient TV. Perhaps it isn't working right. *Still, some warning would have been thoughtful.* To be fair, for her to have come and set everything up during the 15 minutes I was showering is impressive. I had even seen her zapping some pizza rolls in the microwave before I went upstairs maybe twenty minutes ago. My thoughts are stunted as I step out of my walk-in, and my vision absorbs what is playing across the screen.

I see an infant version of myself being rudely poked and prodded by my three older siblings. A heavy lump swells in my throat, as I take a seat on the carpet next to my little sister. It is the first time I have seen Elizabeth in motion since she died.

Delilah admits to tearing up the attic looking for this abundance of home videos. Turns out, my mom is not that stereotypical. The tapes were in the cabinet directly next to the living room television. I had known they were there since she had stopped taping them. I simply could not find the will to watch one. None of us could. With the exception of Delilah, I guess.

Delilah has now forced me to do what I imagined to be torturous. I thought it would be emotionally excruciating to watch Lizzie be the person she no longer is.

The concept seemed agonizing, but the execution makes me feel lighter. She is not a monster who purposefully destroyed our family. She was simply mortal. Her death may have been tragic and preventable, but Elizabeth was just as vulnerable as anybody to the inevitable.

With Delilah's blessing, I decide to bring some of these videos with me to college. I also decide it is time to call Marie.

I gallop downstairs to grab our home phone. I trip over the last step causing me to drop Tommy, whom I was caring. The cat stalks away, definitely holding a grudge. *I'll make amends later*. I continue to the kitchen where I retrieve the sticky note I had copied the number onto from Evan's mobile and begin dialing. I pace as far as the curly cord will allow me as I listen to the distinct buzzing of an outward call. I have no idea if I want her to pick up or not. The ringing drags on. *I should have written a letter.*

Right before the call forwards to their answering machine, I am greeted by a soft, "Hello?"

"Hi," I reply. "Mrs. Creed?"

"This is she," Marie assures.

"This is June Wilson. The intern from Maze Estates. I need to talk to you about something." My heart races as my courage builds.

I tell her everything I can recall that gives me the impression that Randall's suicide is not without blame. I make every effort to be sensitive, but I need her to understand. Marie does not deserve to think that her son took his life at random. He was being suppressed. He should have been able to go home; it was all Randall wanted. I knew her pain was fresh, but that was crucial. It needed to drive her anger. I talk, and she cries, but I keep going.

I recap Randall's initial telling of his story to me. How bleak he felt his future was. I tell her about our last conversation. How unfair his situation seemed. How the obscene amount of guilt on him was thickened, and practically criminalized, by being locked away. I describe my argument with the emotionless women at Randall's funeral. I let her know Michael's insights.

Eventually, I run out of words to say. The weeping on her end becomes silencing. "I'm sorry, Mrs. Creed. I'm so sorry for laying this on you. I just cannot stand knowing a terrible injustice has been done to your son. I had to let you know in case you wanted to pursue—" Her dial tone cuts me off.

I rest the phone on my home's scraped-up kitchen counter. I slide my back down the wall, so I may sit next to the cool air radiating from the fridge. I pick at a hole in my overly-washed leggings and let my thoughts stab at me. I have no clue how what I just did will affect his family. *I may have destroyed it.*

# CHAPTER TWENTY-FIVE: LOCO

Somethings I can reconstruct are my feelings towards Greg. I do want to forgive my late sister's ex. Or at least try, attempt to hear him out. I emailed Greg, very formally, to ask if he wanted to meet. He agreed, and a couple days before I left for school, we did so.

As I sit in my running car, parked at the local Waffle Mansion, I feel a sense of sentimental sadness creep into my already dread-stricken emotions as I remember the last time Evan and I came here. He had coated his hash browns with a thick layer of ketchup, instead of squirting it on the side, convincing me that he is in fact a psychopath.

I watch Greg as rain runs rampant down my windshield, and water threatens to pour out my eyes. He is sitting at a booth, sipping from a beige mug, his shoulders nervously close to his ears. I take a deep breath and think about how much I love Elizabeth, before pushing myself to leave the solace of my vehicle.

My sister's boyfriend is still a ghost of his former self. He was a football player in high school, 6'3" with exceptional muscle tone. His bouncy ebony locks were always perfectly tousled. His cheekbones defined, and his jawline sharp. Today, he is hunched over. His arms wiry, his hair untouched, and his chin sagging.

"Hi, June," Greg says as he moves to stand up.

I slide in across from him before he can. "Hello, Gregory." *Jesus, June take it down a notch.*

"How are you?" He asks timidly.

"Good... Well trying to figure... Trying to save myself." I tell him, before flagging down the waitress for a sweet tea.

"Oh, are you going to church with Delilah?" He inquires, seeming relieved. *Is he a Bible salesman now, or something?*

"No. I'm trying to save myself from losing sight of who I am, who Elizabeth was, how I felt about her," I explain, hoping Randall would be proud of me for making this attempt.

"I see. So… Lizzie. I guess that is what we are here to talk about." He mumbles, staring at his shaking hands. His sleeve catches on the edge of the table, pulling it back to reveal a slew of horizontal scars.

I start gulping my syrupy tea to hydrate the dry scales that have suddenly compromised my vocals. I feel my anger and hurt melt like butter on hot toast. Seeing the torturous pain in Greg's sullen eyes, that once sparkled, and the purposeful disfigurement of his smooth skin thrusts me into his shoes. For the first time, I think about how it feels to be Greg.

My mind flashes to Evan, us drinking in the car, our ridiculously stupid argument a few weeks later. How could I have been so saturated with blatant hypocrisy? Couples fight, people make mistakes, teenagers consume alcohol. Greg was forced to see paramedics show up, asking about a dying girl, the same girl he had left only a short walk away. Greg had to see the bloody indention of Lizzie's cracked skull, touch her unnaturally sallow skin, look into her tenantless blue eyes, graze her purple from lack of oxygen lips. He had come face to face with his detrimental mistake. Even if they would not have worked out long term, I am sure he loved her just as much as I love Evan. I stifle a gag at the thought of seeing his lifeless body.

I place my hands over Greg's to steady them. "I just never told you that I don't blame you."

"Oh, June." As he trembles, big tears are shaken from his hazel eyes. "I am so sorry. I remember holding Lizzie that night, she was so cold, like fucking ice. And I couldn't. No matter what I did, I could not get her to wake up. I told the police when they said the time, I told them that they were wrong. I had just talked to her, she was upset, but she would be fine. It was just an argument, she was going to get over it. I would put her brains back in, but they wouldn't listen. They took her from me. As they strapped her to the stupid gurney, I laid in the water, knowing I was really the one who took her. From you, from your family, from her future. It was all on me." He buries his head in his palms, his shoulders continue to quiver. *Well the brains*

*comment was an unpleasant surprise, never*
*realized the incident caused them to ooze out.*

"Shhhhhhh. It was an accident. Nobody thinks it's your fault. Only you. Don't let this destroy you. Let her be the only one dead." Keeping my voice from cracking becomes impossible.

Greg takes a deep breath. He is able to muster a small amount of composure. "I am so sorry for what I did to you, June. I can't believe I showed up that day. I was just broken out of my mind; I wanted to die at Lizzie's house. I felt the closest to her there."

Wow, I have never known his reasoning. I feel a heavy cloud of guilt settle upon my chest. Randall had shown me how horrendous it was for me to condescend somebody's cry for help, their desperate search for peace. Randall shed light on how pain alters perception. I should have never been so hard on Greg. He was simply unable to cope and did not want to be on this Earth anymore. A completely heartbreaking desire; one even I have never entertained.

"I am the one who should be sorry," I assure Greg. "I never had the decency to check on you. It was all just so much... So tragic."

"June, I would never hold you accountable to that. You were a kid, you still are. You have every right to hate me, but I am glad you don't."

I nod and move to his side of the booth to embrace him. For the first time, in what I assume to be four years, relief reflects from the green specks that dot his wide irises.

# CHAPTER TWENTY-SIX: NORMAL

So, I have comprised some honorable mentions for my summer at Maze. A handful of patients that I really wish I had gotten the opportunity to shadow, a couple of events that slipped through the cracks, and some lessons learned.

Let's starts with Maze's lovely patients. As mentioned, the majority of the patients at Maze were... well, too insane. They were too dangerous to participate in this experience, and of course, I am beyond grateful for Randall. Pearl and Glinda, however... eh. Think I would have preferred one of the following:

Uncle Jiminy. Okay, his real name was Jason Jenning. Jiminy was the name his cult, "Racoons Are Food, Not Friends", called him. These folks were arrested at Yosemite. They had nailed the mutilated carcass of a heavy-set raccoon to a sequoia tree. It was meant to be a "heads up" to its fellow animal that they would soon be feasted upon. I do not know if they caught more critters, but they did make an entire boy scout troop wet their pants.

The group was arrested, most getting nothing but a slap on the wrist. Jiminy, however, was diagnosed with schizophrenia, when he mistook his chubby cellmate for a hormone pumped raccoon and tried to gut him with a plastic spork. Jiminy spent a brief six-month period at a psychiatric ward in California that dealt with patients facing criminal charges. Then he was sent to Maze, as his closest living kin lives in Alabama, and Jiminy has been deemed to be "stable enough."

I only saw the man, who is in his mid-forties, a few times because he was not allowed to go on field trips or attend the crafts room as portraits of pets and wilderness inflame his rage. He looks like if Billy Ray Cyrus and Sean Penn had a child together, that they first tried to abort. *Yikes*. The staff at Maze allow him to wear a raccoon skin cap, which amuses me to no end.

Next, we have Benjamin. Everybody called him Bare Benny because he was addicted to streaking. I witnessed it once. I was trying to ignore Victoria as we were walking in the same direction, one humid day in July. Benjamin was wheel-chairing himself down the hall, but when he saw us, he put an abrupt halt on his roll and stood up. He looked at me and Victoria, before grinning seductively and starting a striptease. He is a big man, about 275 pounds. The fluorescent lights gleamed onto his shiny bald head as he pulled on the edge of his egg-shell colored cotton-tee. He turned his face to the side, his pointer finger in front of his pursed lips as he looked forward once more, making an "oops" face.

As Bare Benny pulled his shirt down his body, the fabric making an audible rip in protest, his sweats were taken too. Victoria and I gawked at his tighty-whities in fearful anticipation. Unable to look away; we could not move so much as a muscle. "Is it just me or is it getting hot in here?" He whispered in a sultry tone. What is revealed by the shedding of his underwear implies that the room is actually quite cold. Benjamin suddenly takes off after us in a sprint, howling at the top of his lungs, his arms stretched above his head, his hands dangling back and forth. We mirror his scream as we turn on our heels. Just as Miranda rounds the corner and tackles him. They hit the ground hard. He was removed from Maze later that day.

Speaking of howling, was Dog-Boy a treat. Oh, and did he love treats. As his name implies, this kid, only a few years older than me, decided he was a dog, a rat-terrier to be more exact. Before voluntarily checking into Maze, he would regularly paint his face and wear a white, fluffy jumpsuit. I saw him at outdoor time almost every day. He adored it. Dog-Boy would gallop on all fours, feeling the wind breeze through his non-existent fur.

Some of the patients, bless their hearts, really did think him to be an actual puppy. I heard one woman say, "my granddaughter told me about companion animals. I am so glad Maze finally got one." Many would even throw sticks for Dog-Boy to go fetch. The reason we interns were not allowed to study him was that he once bit an orderly who tried to take a chicken-wing bone away from him after he had been gnawing on it for half-an-hour.

Then there was Roger. He went crazy after his family was killed by an axe murderer. Yeah, that story doesn't have a funny undertone.

Finally, there was Merlin, "the great sorcerer." I admired Merlin, he was a dreamer. Another voluntary patient, Merlin spent his days spinning down the hall or tossing gravel or "magic dust" in the yard. In the craft room, he created the most exquisite wizard hats out of construction paper. Merlin had a contagious smile and only spoke in riddles. He put an infertility hex on a particularly grumpy nurse, which resulted in the termination of his eligibility for participation in the internship program. I, however, took a liking to the creative bloke. One time, on a field trip to a local rest stop, Merlin sat next to me for the ride there. "Bid thee thy name, mage."

"Uhhh June." I stammered. "You are Merlin, right?"

"Aye, so thy has heard of my mystics. Thou art representative of the month of sun and sacrifice." He informed me while running his fingers through my copper hair.

"Thank you," I responded, finding him to be quite sweet. "I like your sparkly robe. So, what are your thoughts on Mordred? I mean who the hell does he think he is?"

Merlin's eyes glittered with excitement. For thou hath not known thy to be a die-hard King Arthur fan.

Which leads me to my conclusion, being different does **not** make you crazy. How heartbreaking that Merlin felt so apart from society that he should check himself into an asylum. Why are the unique treated with such animosity?

Over the course of two months, I witnessed a lot. Some of it was quite ludacris, I mean I am not saying Jiminy Anti-Racoon Manson or Birthday Suit Ben should be out and about but are they even being helped? Or are they simply being isolated and confined, driving them to a state of further madness?

Insanity is an epidemic. One we all suffer from. So why do we act so cold to the mentally ill? Why is cheating on your wife more acceptable than eating glue? Yes, the idea is humorous, but consider how insignificant an ounce of non-toxic adhesive is to destroying an entire family. Seems odd that victims of trauma, chemical imbalances, and PTSD are cast to the side while the real monsters of humanity live and breathe beside us.

As a result of my sharply winding, vigorously draining, and intoxicatingly rewarding summer, I can no longer indulge in the want for normalcy; the sweet taste of lunacy has become far more crave-able.

# EPILOGUE

Why does announcing that you are going off to University sound so much better than saying I am leaving for college? Is it because University sounds more prestigious? I suppose. Either way, you are traveling to a land of people attempting to find themselves. The great thing about that is that while everyone is trying to place themselves in society, none of them are judging you. That concept in itself already makes college a trillion times more enticing than high school.

The process of my parents and Addison moving me into my dorm turns out to be a tad awkward. Delilah cannot come because she has already started school. *Sucker.* Addison is pregnant again. I have no idea until she confesses during the car ride to Auburn. Because of this, she is omitted from lifting heavy boxes and excuses herself to go to the restroom every few minutes. My parents had seen each other a few weeks prior when they came to

Tuscaloosa for Randall's funeral. I think setting up my dorm together so soon after that is a little more than they can handle. They are ferociously feisty towards one another. Eventually, I tell them I can handle everything else by myself. We can just go to dinner, and then they were free to head home. Everyone likes that idea.

My roommate, Stella, does not show up until a few days after I am moved in. I am nervous to be living in such close proximity with somebody I am not related to or even know at all. When Stella gets to school, I am out grabbing a slice of pizza. I unlock my door and jump a foot when I see a stranger sitting on the vacant side of our room. She finds this hilarious.

The first night she is there, I attempt to sneak a candy bar from the stash I made under my bed. It is past midnight, and the crackling of the wrapper sounds incredibly loud. I drop the chocolate in guilt and begin thinking of an apology as a lamp suddenly clicks on. I look over to see Stella sitting up on her bed, beaming at me. Sort of creeps me out. Then she exposes her own stash. Stella pulls two airplane-sized whiskey bottles from under her mattress and tosses one to me.

She motions for me to sit next to her. "I don't want to share my room with a stranger."

That night we discuss... Well, everything. Once we see that we have complimentary thinking patterns and belief systems, we begin sharing more and more. We are not necessarily from similar backgrounds, and we have not gone through the same hardships. She is an only child from a rich family in Tennessee, who always have way too high of expectations for her. She struggled with off and on eating disorders the majority of her life and had morphed back into herself just a couple of years ago.

So, Stella too has her own set of problems. Honestly, I have to giggle a bit when she admits this to me. Not because I find dangerously restrictive diets comical, but on account of how embarrassed she is to say it. I quickly reassure her that I cannot even begin to describe how screwed up I am.

She gives back to this the snide reply, "always great to have two losers in one dorm." From that point on we are genuine friends.

Stella and I pick up a few more pals from the couple parties we force ourselves to attend. As I am pushed up against a fridge, watching a couple of hammered frat guys play beer pong, I lock eyes with two guys and a girl in the opposite corner, also looking bored. I decide to take a chance and drag Stella by the arm as I go to introduce us. The people: Aaron, James, and Lauren are as equally tortured as us. We all go to the local Waffle Mansion in an attempt to salvage the night.

Aaron, James, and Lauren are a few years older than me, and therefore mature. I can hardly believe I am engaging in actual adult conversations with people around my age. I have finally reached the point in life where everyone is growing up. These fresh friendships are such a strong way to mark that transition. After that night, we exchange numbers and begin hanging out a couple of times a week.

Once classes are in session, I am relieved to

even make a more few friends. I'm just on a roll, now aren't I? Okay, let me take a step back. I am making decently close acquaintances in my classes that I hope to someday call friends. That's more accurate, but still, it's a start!

I am far from fixed. I lose control and cry more than I care to admit. I am sure I annoy the hell out of my newfound friends with the rants and need for emotional support, but they understand. Life is hard and repeating that statement does not make it any easier. Pushing my sarcastic self through though and trying harder and harder to gain a little appreciation for the world, has been a good way to make it less difficult, and more enjoyable.

I have given up on the whole not elaborating on my past to people charade. I am as much of myself as my social anxiety will allow me to be. I realize that I should show appreciation for the relationship I had with Elizabeth because it was not a waste and should not put a fog of negativity on my mindset.

For the next few months though, I still cannot bring myself to think about Randall. Much less talk about him. Every night, I feel a pang of gnawing guilt, knowing that I have wounded his family deeper. I feel like his mom hates me. That I have disrespected Randall's memory. That is until I find out about the Creed's lawsuit.

Do I read about it in the paper? Nope. Do I hear it as gossip? Absolutely not. The Creed's have received a million-dollar settlement for pursuing a case centered on the negligence of their son's mental health through government evaluations.

Later on, I will find out that the largest portion

of the money was given to Randall's friend Simon's wife and daughter. Another sum was divided between the families of the other two men killed in the same incident. With that money, a sizeable trust fund is set up for Randall's sister to have once she turns eighteen. His brother, who is of age, received money as well. But how do I find out about the whole ordeal before knowing any of these details? Because one day, the head of financial affairs at Auburn University summons me to his office.

I am terrified, sure I am in trouble. I feel like a kindergartener being sent to the principal. I tiptoe into the man's office and see him perched in a large, intimidating chair. I take a seat across from him, in one that seems a thousand times lower, as I brace myself for whatever he is about to say.

"Miss Wilson, I have something here I think you might want." A tidal wave of confusion crashes into my mind as these words sound from his sturdy voice. I then notice an open envelope and a rectangular piece of paper lying on the table in front of him.

"Our department received a pretty sizable check this morning. It was made out to you." I immediately prepare myself to find out it is a mistake.

"I guess Mr. Creed, the person it is signed by" *Minor inhale of shock as I think Randall has mailed it from beyond the grave, before realizing his father is also Mr. Creed.* "was nervous about sending such a sizable check to a student's P.O. Box or they are trying to make sure you understand what the check should be used for as it does say 'Tuition' on the bottom. Miss Wilson, I have never had this happen, but the check is in your name. It is yours." He hands me the slip. I feel my eyes widen at the zeros on it.

"Miss Wilson as long as you do not partake in many major changes, or do any slacking off, that check may very well cover your overall cost of attendance here at Auburn. Use it wisely." He instructs. I am in shock. I simply nod and thank him, my mouth hanging open the whole time like a thirsty pup.

I stumble back to my dorm, trying to piece this puzzle together. I am intercepted by a boy, wearing a sideways hat, who is also approaching my room.

"You're June, right?" The wanna-be-gangster asks. I again nod, and he places a package into my bewildered hands. "Cool, this is for you."

Once safely in my dorm, I place the parcel on my bed. I stare at it in curious anticipation before tearing into the thick brown paper, gently. My fingers tremble as I hope I will not damage anything inside. The wrappings cascade to the floor, revealing the enclosed image. I am looking at a painting that depicts a snow-covered forest. I gasp as I realize it is the same picture Randall was painting the day I met him.

Tucked into the corner of the frame, is a folded piece of paper. I flatten it out and begin to read,

Dear June,

Randall had this painting in his room at the time of his death. There was a note on it saying it was for June Wilson. I was selfish and could not part with any piece of my baby. It is now that I understand that this picture needs to belong to you. It's what Randall wanted. I hope it will always have a place to hang in your home.

Much love,

Marie Creed

P.S: The last time I came to visit Randall over the summer, he told me talking to you made him feel like he wasn't crazy. I can never thank you enough for giving my son that solace, even if it was but for a moment.

My breath has been stolen. I stand there for what has to be hours, just remembering the good in my summer at Maze. Eventually, I hear Stella waltz through the door. "Hey, girly. Cool art! We still heading to study group tonight? Don't forget it's Thursday."

"Yeah," I mumble while fighting back tears. "Let's go!"

Stella seems to sense that I need a little push. She slips her arm through mine and begins guiding me into the hallway. Just as my body is about to pass through the door's threshold, I feel my cell phone buzzing in my coat pocket.

"Hold on!" I tell her as I pull it out and open the text message.

It is from Evan. All it says is, *how would you describe Maze on a job application haha.* I chuckle aloud, having no clue how to respond.

## CAROLINE C. COLE

Caroline feels awkward talking about herself in the third person, so she is going to take it from here. I am a 21-year-old Georgia peach bringing you snide and quirky literature one book at a time. I believe in raw content accented with sharp technique. Known to family and friends as "the sweetest psycho you will ever meet", I am an avid dark tourist, meaning I have an interest in morose attractions. Apart from traveling, I am a cat-loving, crime-junkie who adores her family and eats ice cream for breakfast.